LOWCOUNTRY SECRETS, BOOK 2

TYORA MOODY

TYMM PUBLISHING LLC

The Reckoning
Lowcountry Secrets, Book 2

Paperback ISBN: 978-1-961437-32-6

Ebook ISBN: 978-1-961437-31-9

Published by:
Tymm Publishing LLC
www.tymmpublishing.com

Editing: Felicia Murrell
Cover Design: TywebbinCreations.com

Part One

The Escape

Chapter 1

Atlanta, Georgia
Thursday, June 5 at 11:48 p.m.

Katrina Bowen stared at the stranger in the mirror. A tear formed in the corner of her eye and slowly slid down her face. Before she knew it, more tears flowed until her high cheekbones shined. She lifted her right hand to touch her hair.

What was left of it.

What have I done?

She ran her hand over the dark, short natural curls that remained.

He took everything from me!

Katrina turned away from the mirror and swiped at her face as if she could remove the memories of the past few months. Taking a deep breath, her eyes fell on the honey blonde locs strewn across the bathroom floor. Her signature look had earned her over two hundred thousand followers across her social media platforms.

@KatsGlowUp. That's who she'd been. Who everyone knew her as on Instagram, YouTube and TikTok.

She'd spent countless hours recording and then editing short and long form videos. After years of posting black hair care and beauty product reviews, the sponsorship deals poured in. She'd met her goal of becoming a bona fide content creator. No more nine-to-five jobs for her. At twenty-seven, she'd been at the top of her game, establishing herself as a well-known influencer. Katrina had contemplated deleting it all. But why go to that extreme? Instead, she deactivated her accounts, hanging on to a thread of hope.

But *she* had to disappear. Now!

She swallowed hard as she gathered up the locs placing them into a plastic bag. Katrina had stripped down so much of her life the past few days. Last week, she'd paid the last four months on her apartment's lease, telling her landlord she was moving for work. Katrina had loved that place so much she'd started another YouTube channel a year ago. Sharing her bargain store finds and DIY projects with her followers had brought immense joy.

She'd been living her dream.

Then *he* came into her life.

Julian Cross.

The thought of his name made her head throb. Tears welled up in her eyes again, but she had to pull it together. Now wasn't the time to fall apart.

She had to get out of here. Before he knew she'd left Atlanta.

"Kat? Are you okay, honey?"

Startled, she turned around to find her aunt Lola standing in the hallway dressed in her white robe. Despite the late hour and being fifty-three, Aunt Lola still moved with the grace of a dancer. Her legacy made the Lola Davis Dance Academy the most prestigious training facility in the South.

"Your hair," her aunt covered her mouth with her hand.

"It was time for a change." Katrina forced lightness she didn't feel into her voice.

Lola's eyes narrowed. "You've been holed up in the guest room all week. Barely eating. And now this. What's really going on?"

"Trying something new, Auntie. That's all. You've worn your hair short for years." Katrina had always loved how feminine her aunt kept her short, natural hair, now a salt and pepper mix of tight curls.

Lola shook her head. "No! It's *that* man, isn't it? When he came by the house on Monday, I knew something was wrong."

Fear rose up in Katrina's throat.

Because he'd tracked her here.

Still clutching the bag with her shorn locs, Katrina moved past her aunt toward the guest bedroom. She had condensed her entire life into a tote bag and two suitcases. The ring lights, the camera equipment, the packages that had once flooded her apartment, she'd donated or sold. She'd even gotten rid of shoes and clothes, only keeping apparel she couldn't bear to give away.

"Katrina Noelle Bowen." Her aunt followed her into the room. "Talk to me. What is going on?"

Katrina stuffed the bag into the small trash can by the door. Her stomach lurched, as if she'd thrown away something precious. "It's better if you don't know." Her voice came out sharper than she intended. The less her aunt knew, the better.

Aunt Lola crossed her arms, her eyebrows raised. "You made Julian seem like such a nice young man. Did something change?"

Katrina's jaw clenched. A year ago, the first time she'd met him at an influencer gala, Julian *seemed* nice. The charming tech entrepreneur had been featured in *Forbes* and given TED talks about innovation. She couldn't believe *the* Julian Cross had been interested in her. He'd opened her world, introducing her to places and things that she never experienced.

But over the last few months, she'd discovered the real Julian Cross.

That version scared her.

"Auntie, please. I can't talk about this right now. I appreciate you letting me crash here this week, but I need to go."

"Go where?" Aunt Lola let her arms fall to her sides. "Well, will you at least let me know you're okay once you get where you're going?"

"Of course." Katrina pulled the prepaid phone from her pocket, one of three she'd bought with cash at different stores across the city. "I'll call you," Katrina set the small, plain phone in her aunt's hand. "On this phone only."

Her aunt's eyes widened at the unfamiliar phone. "Katrina, what did that man do to you?"

Katrina almost put her fingers to her lips as if to shush her aunt, but she didn't want to alarm her aunt any further. The last thing Katrina wanted to do was to pass along the paranoia that had consumed her over the past few months. It was enough that Julian had been here, at her aunt's house, looking for Katrina. She knew what he could do. The last thing she wanted was to get her aunt involved in the mess Katrina had gotten into.

"Auntie, I promise I'm handling it. This..." She pointed to the infamous burner phone. How often had she seen one of these on television or read about them in a book? "I can't leave a digital trail. Nothing he can... track."

Aunt Lola held her hands to her chest. "Track! I don't understand any of this. Kat, you're scaring me."

Katrina grabbed her aunt's hand. "I'm just being careful. That's all. I'll call in a few days to let you know I'm safe."

Aunt Lola shook her head. "And what am I supposed to tell people when they ask about you? What happens to all the people who follow you on the internet? People at church?"

Katrina shrugged. She couldn't be concerned with people right now. Her goal was to get away from one person. "Tell them I'm taking a break. Mental health and all that. Everyone will understand."

Besides, her mental health had gone downhill, and she couldn't take it anymore.

Her aunt studied her face for a long moment. "I don't like this."

"Believe me, I don't either." Katrina hugged her aunt.

The older woman who'd served as her surrogate mother wrapped her arms around her, hugging her so tight, Katrina almost couldn't breathe.

"Auntie, I need to go." She stepped back, reached down and grabbed the large tote bag, swinging it over her shoulders. Then she wheeled the two suitcases out into the hallway. Her aunt silently followed behind her toward the front door.

Katrina turned to face her aunt. Tears stung her eyes again at the sight of the woman who'd been her rock since Katrina lost her parents. Fifteen years old, scared and angry at the world, but this woman lifted her up, encouraged her, and even disciplined her.

In some ways, Katrina felt like she'd let her aunt down.

Let her parents down.

Somehow she'd missed something in all the training and advice, getting sucked in by a man who could destroy her.

Her aunt touched her shoulder. "Call me when you can. Even if it's just for a minute. I will pray for you. I know God will watch over you."

It was pitch black except for the light on Aunt Lola's front porch. Katrina dragged the suitcases toward the used black Honda Civic she'd bought with cash three days ago. Nothing that would draw attention. Her silver Audi sat in the dealership lot. Might have even been sold by now.

She loved that car. Her first major purchase on her own.

Funny how the flowers delivered to her apartment after she'd blocked Julian's number hadn't done it. Nor the comments on her posts from fake accounts that knew too much about her daily routine. Not even the photos of her at the coffee shop or the gym, nor those of her walking to her car, clearly showing someone had been following her.

No, the last straw had been realizing Julian had known where she was every moment. Nowhere was safe. Every photo location, every tagged restaurant, every casual check-in. She'd built a map for anyone willing to follow, and Julian had been following. He'd turned her privacy into his personal challenge to penetrate. Even after she stopped actively sharing her location, somehow Julian knew.

Katrina's eyes darted around as if expecting something or *someone* to jump out of the shrubbery that lined her aunt's driveway. She quickly packed up the trunk and then slid into the driver's seat, immediately locking the doors. The car still felt foreign to her. Even though she'd bought it with her own money, it didn't feel like her car. She glanced over to see her aunt had closed her front door. Seeing the shut door, Katrina felt even more alone.

She took a deep breath and started the car's engine. It was already well after midnight when she backed out of her aunt's driveway.

Katrina checked her rearview mirror, constantly looking for signs of being followed. As Atlanta's skyline disappeared, she tried not to think about what she was leaving behind. It wasn't the apartment, the sponsorships, or the followers that bothered her. It was the version of herself she'd struggled to build after losing her parents over a decade ago.

Her identity had been stripped.

Because this all felt like she was starting all over again.

Now who am I?

Chapter 2

Beaufort, South Carolina
Friday, June 6 at 6:30 a.m.

Ben Wyatt watched the sun rise. Not because he had some burning desire to be up at the crack of dawn. Sleep eluded him last night as it had the past three years around this time of year.

June 6.

The day everything changed for him.

He sighed and sat up in bed, feeling much older than thirty-three. The rich aromas from the now percolating coffee maker reached his nostrils. His one vice leftover from his detective days, being a coffee snob. The $350 MoccaMaster had proven to be a worthy investment.

Ben flipped the navy blue duvet off his muscular legs and moved through his usual morning routine. Twenty minutes later, with his stainless steel thermos in hand, he headed outside to his truck. The white Ford F-150 bore a hunter green Wyatt Landscaping Services logo on the driver and passenger side door. Behind the truck was a long trailer with a riding lawn mower and other tools.

The people he'd left behind in his past life would hardly recognize him now. Ben had traded in his suits for t-shirts and jeans. The beard he sported most days would surprise his former colleagues. And while his life had changed drastically, Ben appreciated the peace. Or at least the illusion of it.

He genuinely enjoyed being outside, especially this time of year. There was no need for a pricey gym membership; the grueling work kept him fit and sane.

Ben rolled the windows down, enjoying the cool breeze and the salty scent of the Atlantic ocean. His first landscaping job this morning was at Sweetgrass Bed and Breakfast. The owner, Edna Boyd, always made sure he had a hearty breakfast. Her kind of hospitality was something he had to get used to. But he soon learned you never turned down food, especially a good home-cooked meal.

Those meals were usually the best ones he'd have all week. Ben had been forced to learn how to cook basic dishes since moving from Atlanta. It wasn't like there weren't a plethora of restaurants in Beaufort. He just grew tired of being considered a newcomer to the area and having to answer questions. It didn't help that his single status appealed to certain women where he attended church each Sunday.

By nine o'clock, Ben had finished the front and back lawn of the bed-and-breakfast. Sweat dampened his face and his gray t-shirt despite the cool morning temperatures. He surveyed his work while wiping his face with the red bandana he kept in his pocket. This was the part he loved, seeing the grass in neat, even rows.

He loaded the lawn mower back onto the trailer and then grabbed the string trimmer. All that was left to do was to make sure the edges laid crisp along Miss Edna's flower beds among her hydrangeas and azaleas.

It didn't take him long since the garden mainly was positioned under the large bay window in the front of the house. He was heading back to the return the string trimmer to his trailer when he heard the screen door creak open.

"Benjamin Wyatt, you better not be thinking about leaving without breakfast."

Ben grinned and turned to find Edna standing on the wraparound porch with her hands on her hips. Her silver afro caught the morning sunlight streaming across her porch. Despite her stern tone, warmth radiated from her brown eyes.

He grinned. "Wouldn't dream of it, Miss Edna." Ben made sure he'd secured the mower and other tools on the trailer before climbing the porch steps. He left his work boots on the welcome mat outside.

"You always make the yard look so good. I can't tell you how much I appreciate your services." Edna cooed as she held the screen door open for him.

“I appreciate you giving me the work.” He meant it. Deciding to start over in a new place and with a new business was no easy feat.

Savory scents from the kitchen greeted him as he entered Sweetgrass. He followed Edna past the formal sitting room where guests checked in toward the kitchen. Ben washed his hands before settling at the kitchen table.

His mouth watered as Edna sat a bowl of creamy grits topped with shrimp and andouille sausage in a savory brown gravy in front of him. He bowed his head in prayer before picking up his fork. The first bite made his taste buds happy. “Miss Edna, you’ve outdone yourself.”

Edna grinned. “Glad you like it! What else you got going on today?”

Reveling in the rich flavors that could rival any five-star restaurant, it took Ben a moment to respond. “Got three more jobs lined up today.”

Edna nodded. “Good to hear you’re staying busy.” She reached into her apron pocket and withdrew a white envelope, setting it beside his plate. “That should cover this month, plus a little extra for that fertilizer treatment you did last time.”

“Thank you, ma’am.” He tucked the envelope into his back pocket. With customers like Edna, all his worries about choosing an entrepreneurial path were for naught. He often felt like he didn’t deserve where his life had landed. Especially on a day like today.

Edna had poured herself a cup of coffee and settled at the table across from him. For a moment, she was quiet, her gaze drifting toward the window over the sink.

Ben finished up his meal and pushed away the bowl. He could sense Edna had something to say. The woman had an uncanny way of getting him to open up and talk better than any therapist he'd ever had. Well, he'd only had one. The department counselor his chief insisted he see before being accepted back on the force. That didn't work out too well for him.

Which was why that part of his life was now closed.

Edna started, "I'm so proud of you. You've done really well for yourself."

Ben had to admit, this town had offered him what he needed after walking away from his career as a detective. Edna was one of a few who knew about his background. His other clients mainly knew him as Ben the landscaper.

"This town's been good to me," he said finally. "Better than I probably deserve."

"Nonsense. You deserve every good thing that comes your way." Edna's eyes held his with that knowing look she had. "Today's a hard day, isn't it?"

Ben's jaw tightened. He shouldn't have been surprised she remembered today. This woman might be in her early sixties, he'd guess, but her mind was sharp. Edna had coaxed the story out of him over a homecooked dinner. She'd listened without judgment as he shared how his partner had taken a bullet.

He tightened his hands into fists before releasing them.

Today was the day he lost his partner. His best friend.

Ben murmured, "It's been three years and it hasn't gotten any easier."

"Grief doesn't work on a schedule." Edna stood and moved to the coffee pot, pouring him a fresh cup without asking. "Believe me. I miss my brother so much. But he's not hurting anymore."

Ben nodded. He never met Darrell Boyd, Edna's younger brother. Ben only knew that her younger brother passed away after receiving a Stage IV cancer prognosis while in prison. While Edna had lost her brother, his daughter and grandson had become a part of her life, both living at the bed and breakfast as well.

Edna walked back over behind the island. "I often feel guilty about how my brother suffered. Guilt. It will eat you alive if you let it."

Ben wrapped his hands around the warm mug. "Theo had two kids. A wife who loved him. I can't help but feel it should've been me."

Edna swung around, her face fierce. "The Lord decides when it's our time. Not us. Not even the men who pull triggers."

Ben said nothing. He'd heard variations of this from the department counselor, from his mother, and even from the preacher at Theo's funeral. The words never seemed to penetrate the wall of guilt he'd built around himself.

He'd been going to church.

Nothing took his pain away.

"You know what I think?" Edna continued. "I think Theo would be mighty upset to see you punishing yourself like this. From everything you've told me, he was the kind of man who'd want his partner to *live*, not just survive."

The truth of her words hit somewhere deep.

"I'm trying," Ben smiled. "I'm making yards beautiful, one yard at a time." He'd quoted the slogan underneath his logo.

Edna cackled. "You sure are."

The doorbell chimed from the front of the house. Edna frowned, glancing at the clock on the wall. "I'm not expecting any guests until this afternoon. I wonder if they decided to check in early."

She wiped her hands on her apron and headed toward the entryway.

Ben stood from the table, he had work to do. Even though Edna would tell him not to worry about it, he sat his plate and mug in the sink. As he reached the hallway, he could see Edna holding her door open. Nearer to the door, his eyes glimpsed a young woman standing on the porch.

Her hair was cropped short, barely an inch of dark curls covered her scalp. Large brown eyes darted nervously between Edna and Ben.

Ben was immediately drawn to her face with its high cheekbones and smooth chocolate skin. The look in her eyes triggered his curiosity.

This woman's scared of something. Is it me?

Dressed in his grass-stained clothes, he didn't think he appeared too threatening.

Edna beckoned the woman inside. "Honey, come on into the cool air."

The woman hesitated, glancing at Ben before stepping across the threshold.

He instantly stepped back as she entered, sensing her nervousness.

"I'm Edna, the owner of this place." She glanced over at him. "This is Ben. My landscaper."

He gave the woman a head nod. "Good to meet you. Sorry, I didn't catch your name."

The woman hesitated for a minute. "I'm Kat."

"Good to meet you, Kat. Edna, thank you for breakfast. I'm going to head out."

"Alright, Ben." Edna pointed her finger. "Dinner will be at six."

He snuck a glance at the woman. She was tall against his 6'2. The young woman could have easily been at home on some fashion runaway with those cheekbones and lips.

She is gorgeous!

Ben exited and closed the front door behind him. Even after he cranked up his truck, his mind stayed fixed on the woman he'd briefly met. The younger version of himself used to love to flirt with pretty women, especially when he had his badge. But women always left him when they realized his job was his life.

The way the woman walked in sent Ben's instincts into high alert. He could sense her fear.

Who was she? And who was she running from?

Chapter 3

Beaufort, South Carolina
Friday, June 6 at 9:38 p.m.

Katrina left Atlanta with no real plan. Her only goal was to escape under the cover of darkness. She hadn't slept in days and exhaustion had caught up with her as she passed one marker after the next. The highway stretched endlessly in front of her. Somewhere around three in the morning, she'd pulled to the side of the road, too tired to keep her eyes open. She'd meant to rest for just a few minutes.

Instead, she'd jolted awake an hour later, heart pounding, certain she'd heard footsteps crunching on the gravel outside the car. But no one had been there. Just lots of trees, crickets chirping and the road ahead. It was so dark. Not a single pair of headlights in either direction.

She was alone.

But away from him.

Katrina had thought about heading down to Florida. She swung back on the road, no longer sure she could stay in the car that long. Another hour passed and the sun began to rise.

Her eyes felt gritty from staring through the car's windshield, but Katrina welcomed the orange tinged sky. She drove across the border of South Carolina, still uncertain about where she was going. Her mom had grown up in South Carolina. She'd met Katrina's dad, a Morehouse Man, while she was at Spelman.

Feeling guided by memories from her childhood, Katrina could picture peaceful waves of water. She saw a mile marker for Beaufort, fifty-five miles ahead. She was in Lowcountry, her mother's home. Remembering the long summer drives from their home in Atlanta, even the highway began to look more familiar to her.

Then the sign appeared.

Welcome to Beaufort.

Her hands trembled on the steering wheel. She needed to stop. Her body felt close to breaking down.

When was the last time I ate?

Her appetite had been off for weeks. And she needed to sleep in a real bed. Somewhere safe so she could figure out what to do next.

The downtown area was picturesque with its historic buildings draped in Spanish moss. Katrina caught the glint of water visible between storefronts. Under different circumstances, she might have found it charming. Right now, she was too tired to play tourist.

She guided the car into a residential area. Feeling lost, she kept driving, not sure how she would find a hotel. Katrina glanced down at the gas and saw the lever was dangerously close to empty. Swearing under her breath, panic crept up her back. Up ahead, she caught sight of a two-story Victorian with a wraparound porch and blue rocking chairs. Hanging ferns swayed in the breeze, and flowerbeds burst with color along the front walk.

A wooden sign swung gently in the morning breeze.

Sweetgrass Bed and Breakfast.

A white Ford F-150 sat curbside, a trailer hitched behind it carrying a commercial lawnmower. The grass looked freshly cut. Without thinking, Katrina pulled into the driveway and cut the engine. For a long moment, she sat there, hands gripping the steering wheel. She let go and ran her hands across her hair. The shortness felt unfamiliar. Katrina reached for the rearview mirror. Her eyes widened at her appearance.

She looked nothing like the woman who'd built a following of two hundred thousand people. That woman had been confident and always camera-ready. This tired looking woman looked far older than her twenty-seven years.

Just go inside. Ask if they have a room. You can figure out everything else later.

Katrina grabbed her tote bag and climbed out of the car on unsteady legs. The morning air was thick with humidity. Somewhere nearby, birds were singing.

Her legs wobbled as she climbed the stairs to the porch. A fit woman who loved yoga classes, it was crazy how out of shape she felt after a few weeks. Well, more like a few months.

She rang the doorbell and waited. The door opened, and an older Black woman with a silver afro stood in the entryway. She wore a flour-dusted apron, and her brown eyes were kind. “Can I help you, honey?”

Katrina knew she looked like a hot mess. Undone by the gentleness in those simple words, her throat tightened. She took a deep breath before finding her words. “I’m looking for a room,” she managed. “Do you have anything available?”

The woman studied her for a moment. “Honey, come on into the cool air.”

Behind the older woman, a man stood in the foyer.

Katrina’s breath caught.

He was tall, broad-shouldered, with close-cropped dark hair and skin a shade or two darker than her own. He wore a sweat-dampened gray t-shirt and jeans, grass stains visible on the fabric.

Katrina’s muscles tensed.

Don’t be stupid. You need to go inside.

She forced herself to look away from the man, focusing on the woman's kind face. From her peripheral vision, she noticed the man had stepped back.

Feeling self-conscious, Katrina stepped over the threshold. The interior of the bed-and-breakfast appeared warm and cozy. The faint aroma of something smelled good, taunting Katrina's stomach.

"I'm Edna, the owner of this place." The lady glanced over at the man. "This is Ben. My landscaper."

Ben gave her a head nod. "Good to meet you. Sorry, I didn't catch your name."

Katrina hesitated for a minute. She hadn't talked to anyone in the hours since she left her aunt Lola's home. Should she give her real name? No. It was safer to use her nickname.

"I'm Kat."

The man gave her a warm smile that lit up his handsome face. "Good to meet you." He turned to the woman. "Edna, thank you for breakfast. I'm going to head out."

"Appreciate it, Ben. You enjoy the rest of your day."

He glanced at her again as he walked out the door. Katrina caught his masculine scent mixed with grass.

"How long are you looking to stay?" Edna had walked over to a small desk in the corner of the sitting room.

Katrina scrambled over feeling like she was wading under water. "I'm not sure yet." Her voice sounded distant to her own ears. "A few days, maybe? Is that okay?"

"That's just fine. I think the Blue room will be perfect for you. It's quiet and faces the garden out front." Edna pulled out a registration book. "I'll need your full name for the register."

Katrina hesitated again. She decided to go with her mother's maiden name.

"Kat. Kat Miles."

If Edna noticed the pause, she didn't comment. "Well, Miss Kat, welcome to Sweetgrass. The room is a hundred and twenty a night, includes meals. I can work out a weekly rate if you decide to stay longer."

Katrina opened her bag where a stack of bills laid at the bottom. It was all the money she had for now, and it would have to last because she couldn't bank online. "For now, I'd like to pay for three nights. Is cash alright?"

"Cash is just fine, honey." Edna accepted the bills without question, counting them out before tucking them into the desk drawer. "Now then, when's the last time you ate? Or slept, for that matter? You look about ready to fall over."

"I... I don't know." The admission made her feel vulnerable.

"Let's get you upstairs first. You can bring your things in later, or I can have someone help you—"

"No," Katrina said quickly. "I mean, I can manage. I just need to rest first."

Edna nodded. "Come this way, then."

She guided Katrina toward a curved staircase. The stairs felt endless, each step requiring more effort than the last. By the time they reached the landing, Katrina was swaying on her feet.

“The Blue room,” Edna said, opening a door to reveal a cheerful space with pale blue walls and deeper blue curtains. Sunlight streamed through windows overlooking the front garden. A four-poster bed dominated the room, piled high with pillows and covered in a crisp white quilt.

It was the most beautiful room Katrina had ever seen.

“Bathroom’s through there.” Edna pointed to a door on the right. “Fresh towels are in the cabinet. I’ll bring up something to eat soon. You just rest.”

“Thank you.” The words felt inadequate for what Edna was offering her.

Edna left, pulling the door gently closed behind her. Katrina stood in the middle of the room for a long moment. Through the window, she could see her black Honda sitting in the driveway now. Her suitcases were still in the trunk, but she couldn’t make herself care.

She kicked off her shoes and laid across the mattress with her bag clutched against her chest. The bed felt soft and comforting.

She was safe.

Her eyes drifted closed and sleep overtook her body.

Chapter 4

Beaufort, South Carolina
Friday, June 6 at 11:32 a.m.

Ben guided the edger along Anita Mason Carver's front walk, but his mind was still back at Sweetgrass. The woman looked like she was on the run from something. He'd seen that body language before, back when he wore a badge.

Kat.

Was that her real name?

The way she stepped back, her eyes wide, almost like she was afraid of him. The gesture reminded him of a feline ready to run or strike.

It's none of my business.

There wasn't anything he could do. He hadn't even been able to save his partner. All he could protect now were flowers, grass, and shrubbery. Once the temperatures rose higher, he would struggle to do that for his clients.

Ben had just finished edging around the azaleas when he heard his name. Unlike Edna who greeted him with warm hospitality and a meal, Ben preferred to keep conversation with Anita to a minimum.

He suppressed a sigh before turning around. “Morning, Mrs. Carver.”

She stood at the top of the steps like a queen. At seventy-two, Anita Carver moved with the deliberate grace that belied her true self as the neighborhood gossip. “How’s business treating you?”

“Can’t complain. Staying busy.”

“I saw you were at Edna Boyd’s this morning.” Mrs. Mason settled onto her porch rocking chair as if preparing for a lengthy chat. “She was the one who recommended you to me.”

Ben nodded. “I appreciate both of you.”

“Poor Edna.” Mrs. Mason’s voice. “Can you believe it’s been over a year since Darrell passed?”

Ben looked down the road where he could see the Sweetgrass sign swinging. He hated how Mrs. Carver sneaked into conversations gossip about other people. Her daughter, Michelle Carver, was a realtor and often stopped by to check on her mother, usually when Ben came to do yard work.

Ben wanted to finish his work quickly today. Both mother and daughter liked to play matchmaker, and he was the prize. But Ben didn’t have the capacity today to push himself to be social. Miss Edna made it easy. Other folks just made him tired.

Mrs. Carver continued talking, even though he didn't give her a response.

"Stage IV cancer. Just terrible." Mrs. Carver shook her head. "Of course, some folks say he got what he deserved going to prison, but I never believed that man killed anyone. I'm glad he could have some peace. Put all of that messiness behind him."

Ben busied himself by opening the mower's gas tank, checking the level. Still half full.

"At least Edna has Tracey and little Jayden living with her now," Mrs. Carver said. "Family's important, especially when you're grieving."

The word hit him harder than it should have. Ben's jaw tightened as he closed the gas cap, forcing his hands to remain steady.

Three years today.

"The edging around the beds looks so good." Mrs. Carver commented.

Thankful that the older woman had changed the subject, he smiled. "Glad you like it."

His phone buzzed in his pocket. He pulled it out, wondering if it was a client asking for his services.

His stomach dropped.

Sarah Mason.

"Excuse me, Mrs. Carver. I need to take this."

For a moment, Ben just stared at the screen. Sarah never called unless it was important. Usually she texted. A phone call meant she actually needed to talk.

The phone buzzed again in his hand, her name lighting up the screen.

He walked to his truck, putting distance between himself and Mrs. Carter's prying eyes before answering.

"Hey, Sarah."

"Ben." Her voice was soft, familiar in a way that made his chest ache.

He leaned against the truck bed. "Everything okay? The boys?"

"We're fine. Everyone's fine." There was a long, interminable pause. "I just wanted to check on you."

Ben closed his eyes. Of course she'd call.

"I'm doing okay," he managed. The lie tasted bitter.

"Ben—"

"Really, Sarah. I'm fine. How are you? How are Tony and Tyler?"

Another pause, longer this time. When Sarah spoke again, her voice was careful. "Tyler's good. Made the soccer team. He's excited."

"That's great. Tell him congratulations for me."

"I will." She took a breath. "Tony is... that's actually partly why I called."

Ben's grip on the truck tightened. "Is he alright?"

"He's struggling a bit. It's the anniversary, and he's fifteen now, and..." Her voice wavered slightly. "He's been asking questions. About his dad. About that night."

The words hit like a physical blow. Ben's vision blurred slightly, the bright afternoon sun suddenly too harsh.

"What kind of questions?" His voice came out rougher than intended.

"About what happened. About the case you two were working on. About..." She paused. "About you."

"Me?"

"He wants to understand, Ben. He's old enough now that the simple answers don't work anymore. And he knows you were there. He knows you and Theo were partners."

Ben pressed his free hand against his forehead. Tony was twelve when it happened. Small for his age, obsessed with *Minecraft*, still young enough to believe his dad was invincible. Now he was fifteen, asking questions Ben didn't know how to answer.

"What did you tell him?" he asked quietly.

"The truth. As much of it as I know." Sarah's voice shook. "That his father was doing his job. That he was brave."

Ben's throat constricted.

"Sarah—"

"I'm not calling to make you feel guilty," she interrupted. "I know you carry enough of that already. I'm calling because Tony wants to talk to you. Not now, not right away. But sometime soon. If you're willing."

Ben couldn't speak. His mind flooded with images of Theo laughing at some stupid joke. Theo teaching Tony to throw a curveball. Theo bleeding out on the ground while Ben screamed for help.

The hospital waiting room had fluorescent lights that were way too bright. Ben sat in a plastic chair with Theo's blood still on his hands, his shirt.

Sarah arrived twenty minutes after the ambulance. She took one look at Ben's face and knew.

"No," *she said. Just that one word.* "No."

Ben stood, but he didn't know what to say. There were no words.

The doctor came out around the same time.

Sarah's face crumbled before the doctor even spoke. Ben caught her as her knees gave out.

Help came too late.

"Tony doesn't blame you, Ben," Sarah's voice cracked slightly. "None of us do. But he wants to know about his dad. The parts only you can tell him. The partner stuff. The good days."

"I don't know if I can do that." Ben's voice broke.

"You don't have to decide now. I just wanted to ask. To give you time to think about it." She paused. "He misses you, you know. Both of the boys miss Uncle Ben. We still joke about Uncle Ben's rice."

Ben chuckled, remembering a younger Tony asking him if he was the same guy from the box. Theo had started that nonsense. "I miss you guys, too."

"Take care of yourself, okay?"

"Yeah, you too. And, Sarah, I'll think about it," he said. "Talking to Tony. I just need some time."

"Of course. There's no rush. Call me if you need anything. Even just to talk."

"I will. Tell the boys I said hello."

"I will. Bye."

After she hung up, Ben stood there for a long moment, gripping the phone in his hand. The afternoon was bright and warm. Like he usually did, he looked over his work, inhaling the fresh cut grass.

"Benjamin?"

He jumped, nearly dropping the phone.

Unfortunately, Mrs. Carver hadn't gone into the house. She stood from the porch with an envelope in her hand. "Everything alright over there, dear? "

Ben straightened, shoving the phone back in his pocket. "Yes, ma'am."

Her sharp eyes studied him, but she didn't push. She handed him the envelope. "Good work today. It's going to get hotter. Make sure you stay cool."

"Will do." He took the check and sauntered back to his truck as though nothing was wrong. He'd been going through the motions, the landscaping helping him occupy his mind. The phone call from Sarah was unexpected and not what he needed.

What could I even say to Theo's son?

Ben had been over that night so many times. In his head while awake. In nightmares that ripped him from sleep. If he could have changed places with Theo, he absolutely would have.

Inside the truck, he cranked the engine. He let the cool air blow across his face as he took a swig of water. His next job was across town, a retired couple who wanted their hedges shaped before their grandchildren visited. His route would take him back past Sweetgrass.

As he neared Sweetgrass, movement in the driveway caught his eye. The woman from this morning, Kat. She stood behind her Honda, pulling suitcases from the trunk. She closed the trunk and turned toward the street. Her short hair made her seem small, almost childlike.

Her eyes scanned the street.

Ben's grip tightened on the steering wheel as they locked eyes with one another.

Kat grabbed her suitcases and hurried toward the house, disappearing through the front door before he passed the property line.

Ben frowned as he glanced in the rearview mirror.

Kat, what are you running from?

Chapter 5

Atlanta, Georgia
One Year Ago

Katrina adjusted the thin strap of her gold dress, still not quite believing she was here. The St. Regis Atlanta ballroom glittered like something out of a fairy tale. The Atlanta Influencer Summit's closing gala. Content creators mingled with brand executives and tech gurus.

She'd been excited about her conversation with the head of the upcoming black makeup line, ColorMe. The female CEO wanted her to help launch their products in a month and had given her a swag bag. Katrina loved how well the mocha foundation matched her skin complexion. While rummaging through the bag like a kid in a candy store, she felt someone watching her.

Katrina looked up, her professional smile already in place. Brands had approached her all evening. Showed how far she'd grown from the first time she attended this event. Four years ago, she was approaching brands and pitching to them. Times had changed.

A man stood near the bar, tall and confident in a tailored navy suit. Dark wavy blonde hair, strong jawline, with the kind of smile that looked like it knew a secret. When their eyes met, Katrina couldn't look away.

He was gorgeous, but not her type.

Still, her stomach fluttered when the man crossed the room with two champagne flutes in hand.

"Katrina Bowen." His voice was smooth. "I've been hoping to meet you all night."

She accepted the champagne, trying not to seem as flattered as she felt. "Thank you. You know who I am?"

"Of course."

"And you are?"

"Julian Cross." He extended his hand. "I run a tech startup. We do AI-driven marketing analytics. Boring stuff compared to what you do."

Katrina realized she knew exactly who he was. But tonight, he wasn't wearing his glasses and his hair was slicked back. Usually, his curls fell over one side. She knew he'd been featured in *Forbes* 30 under 30 and became a millionaire by the time he turned twenty-five.

Julian Cross was talking to me.

They talked for an hour. Then two.

He asked about her journey and seemed to be really listening to her answers. She often shared her story on social media about the loss of her parents at age fifteen, how grief almost drove her to the edge. Then she'd started small, talking about and reviewing products she liked on YouTube. It was something for her to do. A way to find her purpose.

"You're remarkable," he said. "Most people talk about their brand. You talk about purpose. Your parents would be so proud of you."

No one had ever said anything like that to her before.

"Can I take you to dinner?" He took her hand. "Tomorrow night? I know this place in Buckhead that's quiet, intimate. Somewhere we can actually talk without all this noise."

She should have said no. Should have remembered her rule about not mixing business with personal life.

But I said yes.

Beaufort, South Carolina
Friday, June 6 at 12:15 p.m.

Katrina jolted awake, gasping.

Her heart hammered against her ribs. Sweat dampened her neck. For a disorienting moment, she didn't know where she was. Her hand squeezed the pillow next to her as a whimper escaped her throat.

Blue walls. White quilt. The smell of lavender. Antique furnishing.

Sweetgrass Bed and Breakfast.

She was nowhere near Atlanta.

Safe. For now.

Katrina pressed a hand to her chest, willing her breath to slow. She reached for the burner phone on the nightstand and squinted at the screen. 12:15 p.m. She'd slept two hours.

Her body still ached, but the much needed nap helped. She swung her legs over the side of the bed and caught her reflection in the dresser mirror. The short curls still startled her. The shadows under her eyes made her look like some zombie. Her first thought was she needed makeup. She looked around.

Oh no, my suitcases!

They were still in the trunk of her car. She'd been so exhausted, she'd collapsed, bringing nothing inside. Katrina splashed water on her face in the small bathroom, rinsed her mouth, and headed downstairs.

She cringed as the old stairs creaked under her feet. Voices drifted up from the foyer. Katrina paused on the landing and peered down to find Edna speaking to a young couple at the check-in desk. There was a pile of luggage near the door, most of it pink.

"The Yellow room has the most beautiful morning light," Edna said as she handed over a key.

"Sounds perfect." The woman clutched the man's arm. "Didn't I tell you? This is exactly what I imagined for our honeymoon."

He kissed her temple. "You were right. As always."

The sight of the young couple made something twist in Katrina's chest. She had been so excited about the possibilities. The beauty influencer with the young tech mogul. Then Julian had shown her how wrong she could be about a man. She'd stumbled in her dating life, but never had she fallen for a full-on narcissistic psychopath.

Hoping Edna didn't notice her, Katrina slipped out the front door. The afternoon heat wrapped around her like a damp blanket as soon as she ventured down the porch steps. Katrina popped the trunk of the Honda and pulled out her two suitcases. She looked around after closing the trunk, breathing in the freshly cut grass. For a moment, Katrina turned her face up to embrace the sun's rays.

The sound of an engine made her direct her eyes to the street. A white truck with a trailer hitched behind it rolled down the street. The same truck from this morning. She remembered the green logo on the door. As the truck passed the driveway, the driver's head turned toward her.

Their eyes met through the windshield. His gaze steady, almost curious.

Katrina grabbed her suitcases and hurried toward the house, her heart pounding harder than it should have. She didn't look back to see if the truck had stopped. The handsome landscaper might be non-threatening, but this past year with Julian had taught her to be weary of men. Especially the good-looking ones.

The trend online about whether a woman should choose the bear or man in the woods. She most certainly would hurl herself toward the bear. At least she knew the big, furry creature's true intentions.

Before she could carry her bags upstairs, Edna appeared in front of her.

"You're just in time for lunch," Edna declared. "I'll fix you something to eat."

"Oh, I don't want you to trouble yourself." Katrina's stomach growled loudly, and she dropped her shoulders, embarrassed by the betrayal.

Edna's eyebrows rose. "That settles it. Set those bags in the corner behind the check-in desk and follow me."

Katrina hesitated, but Edna was already heading toward the kitchen, clearly expecting her to follow. She left her bags where requested and headed toward the doorway where Edna had disappeared.

The kitchen was large and warm, clearly the heart of the house. Copper pots hung from a rack over a center island. Herbs grew in small terracotta pots on the windowsill. Late afternoon sunlight streamed through lace curtains, casting patterns on the quaint wooden table.

Edna gestured to a chair at the table. "Sit. I made chicken salad this morning, and I have some nice croissants from the bakery downtown."

Within minutes, a plate appeared before her. A buttery croissant stuffed with creamy chicken salad dotted with grapes and pecans, alongside fresh strawberries and a handful of red grapes. Edna poured iced tea in a tall glass and sat it next to the plate.

Katrina's mouth watered before she picked up the chicken salad sandwich. She took a bite. The flavor combination exploded in her mouth. She closed her eyes, suddenly overwhelmed by how good it was. Her appetite had been destroyed the past few weeks.

She ate faster, then caught herself, embarrassed. "I'm sorry. This is incredible."

Edna waved off the apology. "Nothing to be sorry for. A woman needs to eat." She settled into the chair across from Katrina, setting down her own glass of tea. "Where are you traveling from, Kat?"

Katrina swallowed. "Georgia."

"What brings you to Beaufort?"

She'd not prepared for these questions and answered as honestly as she could. "My mother grew up in the Lowcountry. I used to visit when I was young." The truth, if not the whole truth. "Both of my parents passed away over ten years ago. I guess I wanted to feel close to her again."

Edna's expression softened. "I'm sorry, honey." She paused, her gaze drifting toward the window. "I lost my brother last year. Cancer. It's still fresh."

"I'm sorry."

Edna took a sip of her tea. "Grief has its own timeline. Can't rush it, can't outrun it. All you can do is keep putting one foot in front of the other."

Katrina nodded slowly. She wasn't just grieving for her parents, though. She was grieving the life she'd built. The woman she used to be.

"You got family waiting for you somewhere?" Edna asked.

"It's just me now." Katrina pushed the plate away. When she looked up, Edna was watching her with kind eyes.

"Thank you for the meal."

Edna smiled and stood. "No problem. Dinner will be at six. As long as you're here, you don't have to worry about meals."

Katrina felt something loosen in her chest as she left the kitchen. It felt like she could breathe more freely again, as if recovering from a long illness. She grabbed her suitcases from the sitting room and headed upstairs. She could hear the couple unpacking, but all she could see when she passed by were pale yellow walls. That had to be the Yellow room.

Katrina liked the color coordination of the rooms and wondered how many other bedrooms were in the bed-and-breakfast. She closed and locked her door, this time really taking in the Blue room. She'd done something similar. Her second YouTube channel really delved into her color-matching and other decoration adventures for each room in her apartment.

She sighed and began unpacking, starting with her small bag of toiletries. Katrina loved that the bedroom had its own bathroom. While she wasn't fully committed to staying more than a few days, she placed a few clothes in the dresser drawers. She'd given little thought about what to do next.

At the bottom of her tote bag, her fingers found the five by seven frame. She pulled it out carefully. In the past decade, this photo of her parents had gone everywhere with her. She always sat it on her nightstand. Taken only a few days before the car accident that killed them both, her mother smiled, looking up at her father. He had a protective arm around her shoulder. Katrina had taken the photo herself, not knowing it would be the last one she'd ever snap.

Katrina set the photo on the nightstand, touching each of her parent's faces through the glass. "I'm here in the Low-country, Mama. I don't know what to do next, but I made it this far."

She reached back into the tote bag and pulled out one of the burner phones. She'd promised Aunt Lola she'd call. She dialed the number she'd memorized to the matching burner she'd pressed into her aunt's hand.

Was that just last night?

Loneliness and despair crept into her mind, it felt like her last conversation with Aunt Lola had been days ago. Everything blurred in her mind.

The phone rang twice before Aunt Lola's breathless voice came through. "Kat? Baby, is that you?"

The sound of her aunt's voice cracked something open in Katrina's chest. It took her a few seconds to open her mouth. "It's me, Auntie. I'm safe."

"Thank God." She could hear her aunt exhale. "I've been carrying this phone everywhere. Checking it every five minutes like a crazy woman. Where are you?"

"I can't say exactly. But I found a place to stay. A bed-and-breakfast in a small town. The owner is..." Katrina paused, thinking of Edna's kind eyes. "She's good people."

"Are you eating? Sleeping?"

"I just had the best meal I've had in weeks. And I slept a little."

Silence stretched between them.

"Has he—" Katrina started.

"No." Lola's voice hardened. "And if he shows up here again, I've got my Louisville Slugger ready."

"Auntie."

"I mean it. That man comes near my property again. He'll find out this dancer still has her swing."

Alarm bells that had triggered Katrina for months started clanging. "Don't engage with him. Please. He's dangerous, Auntie. More than you know."

"I gathered that much when my niece showed up at my door looking like a ghost and left in the middle of the night with burner phones." Lola paused. "Baby, are you sure you don't want to go to the police? Whatever he did—"

"The police can't help me." Katrina closed her eyes. Julian Cross was a giant, and she was nothing.

"I don't like this," Lola hissed. "I don't like any of this."

"I know. Neither do I." Katrina touched her parents's photo on the nightstand. "But I'm handling it. I just needed you to know I'm okay."

"You call me again soon, you hear? Don't make me wait, wondering if you're alive."

"I will. I promise."

"I love you, Katrina Noelle."

"I love you too, Auntie."

Katrina ended the call and set the phone on the nightstand. The brief connection to her old life left her feeling hollowed out and homesick.

She lay back on the bed, staring at the ceiling. Outside her door, she could hear the young couple moving down the hall, then down the stairs. Probably going to explore the town. This place was nice from what she could remember from her childhood. She would love to explore it like a tourist.

But she wasn't some tourist.

Tomorrow, she would figure out her next move. For now, she would close her eyes and let herself rest.

Chapter 6

Lady's Island, South Carolina
Friday, June 6 at 4:47 p.m.

The crushed shell driveway crunched beneath Ben's tires as he pulled up to his uncle's property. Live oaks draped with Spanish moss framed the modest ranch house, their branches creating a canopy of green and gray.

He sat in the truck for a moment, letting the AC blow across his face. The day had wrung him out. Uncle Vern's yard was his last job of the day. Though Ben never charged, his father's oldest brother insisted on paying anyway. They'd had the same argument for three years now. Today, Ben didn't have the energy to fight with his stubborn uncle. Instead, he was grateful he'd started and ended his workday with two of his favorite people in this town.

He unloaded the mower from the trailer and got to work. Usually the familiar rhythm up and down the lawn soothed him. After the phone call from Sarah, he'd been unable to hide within his work today. His mind circled back to that day three years ago.

Theo's oldest son was twelve back then, the same age Ben had been when Uncle Vern sat him down before his father's funeral. Ben hadn't wanted to go. He didn't want to see the man he'd admired in a coffin, gone forever.

Your daddy was a hero, Ben. Don't ever let anyone tell you different.

He remembered his uncle's heavy hand on his shoulder. The way Vern's voice had cracked. Ben had nodded along, not really listening.

He'd lost his hero. Just like Tony.

No one understood why Ben enrolled in the police academy. His mother was heartbroken that her baby boy had followed in his dad's footsteps. Ben's older brother, David, said Ben was smart and should be a lawyer like him. His sister, Patrica, was just as incredulous, suggesting Ben be a doctor like her. But somehow the academics of it all hadn't appealed to him. He'd always wanted to be like his father. It had been a way for him to keep the memory of the man alive.

Ben finished the front yard and moved to the back, pushing through the work despite the thoughts warring in his mind. By the time he killed the mower's engine, sweat had soaked through his shirt again. He could smell the grass, dirt and odor on himself. A good hot shower was what he needed.

After Ben loaded the mower onto the trailer, his uncle emerged on the back porch carrying two glasses of lemonade. At seventy-one, Vernon Wyatt still carried himself like a man who'd worn a badge for thirty years. Tall, broad-shouldered, with close-cropped gray hair and a neatly trimmed mustache, he moved slower than he used to, but his eyes were still sharp.

Uncle Vern eyed him. "Gonna be a hot one tomorrow."

Ben wiped his face with the red bandana from his pocket, covering a smile. His uncle always started conversations as if they'd just been talking. "Yes, sir."

"You gonna come sit?"

Ben hopped up on the porch and took the lemonade before grabbing a seat in the rocker next to the one where his uncle sat. Vern rocked slowly, looking out over the yard. The silence stretched between them, but it wasn't uncomfortable.

Vern broke the silence first. "How you doing today? Seemed like you got a lot on your mind."

Ben took a long drink of lemonade. The tartness cut through the thickness in his throat. "Good. Had plenty of work today."

"Mmm. Your mama called me this morning," Vern continued. "Wanted to make sure I'd check on you."

Of course she did.

Ben looked up and then sighed deeply.

Gloria Wyatt had been worried about her youngest son since he left Atlanta. She called every Sunday after church, asked the same questions he never fully answered. David thought Ben was running from his problems, and Patricia sent care packages he didn't need and texts he didn't always return.

He knew they loved him, but they didn't understand why he left.

"I'm fine," Ben responded. "Told her that last Sunday."

Vern grunted. "Boy, that's what mamas do. They worry about their children. Be glad your mama is still around. There are days I wish I could still see and hear mine."

Ben swallowed. Then he blurted, "Sarah called today."

Vern's rocking chair stilled. "Theo's wife?"

"She wants me to talk to Tony. Their oldest." Ben stared out at the freshly cut grass, seeing none of it. "He's fifteen now. Asking questions about that night. About his dad."

Vern was quiet for a moment. "What kind of questions?"

"The kind I don't know how to answer."

"That boy misses his father." Vern stated. "Not just how he died."

Ben looked at his uncle. The older man stared back at him, reminding him of that moment long ago.

Vern set his lemonade on the small table between the rocking chairs. "Your mama was in no shape and asked me to talk to you. You weren't talking at all. Completely silent. Refusing to go to the funeral."

Ben remembered sitting in his room staring at the suit his mama had laid out for him. The last thing he wanted was to put on that tight suit.

"I didn't know what to say," Vern admitted. "Had this speech in my head about duty and sacrifice and how your daddy died protecting people." He shook his head slowly. "Soon as I saw your face, I forgot all of it."

Ben's grip tightened on the glass of lemonade. "What did you tell me? I can't remember exactly."

Vern was silent for a long moment, his eyes distant. "I told you your daddy loved you more than the job. That was the truth. John lived for you kids, and for your mama. The badge was what he did, but y'all were his world."

Ben's throat constricted.

"And I told you it was okay to be angry," Vern continued. "At him, at God, at whoever. Because I was angry too. Mad as hell that my little brother was taken from us."

Ben said quietly. "I stayed angry a long time."

Vern picked up his glass again. "You were a bit out of control in school for a while. Everybody was angry you went to the academy. I knew it was good for you. That discipline. You needed purpose."

Ben stared at his feet. His uncle was right about following his purpose.

Then he walked away from it.

Vern clasped his hands in his lap. "You know, law enforcement runs in the Wyatt family. Your granddaddy was a Fulton County Sheriff's deputy for twenty-two years. Your daddy in the Atlanta PD. I went a different direction, stayed here in Beaufort County. Nice quiet place. Thirty years I gave to it.

Saw things I still can't shake. But I made it out. Retired. Got to grow old with my Della."

His voice dropped. "I know it's hard because your daddy didn't get that chance. Neither did Theo."

Ben's throat tightened.

"That boy doesn't need you to have all the answers," Vern said. "He just needs to know someone remembers his daddy. Someone who was there."

"I was *there* when he died, Uncle Vern." Ben's voice cracked. "I watched him—"

Vern reached out a gnarled hand, pointing his finger. "You don't tell him that part. You tell him about the man Theo was before that night. The partner. The friend. The way he probably talked too much and laughed too loud and drove you crazy half the time."

Ben chuckled. Theo talked way too much. Told the worst jokes. Sang off-key to the radio during stakeouts. Could eat his weight in wings and still want dessert.

"That's what the boy needs," Vern said. "Not the last five minutes. The years before."

Ben let the words settle. They made sense, the way Uncle Vern's words usually did.

The screen door opened behind them, and Aunt Della appeared. She was a warm, round-faced woman in her late sixties with silver-streaked hair pinned back in a bun. She peered at Ben over her reading glasses, which were perched dangerously at the end of her nose.

"Benjamin Wyatt, are you staying for dinner? I'm making smothered pork chops, and you know I always make too much."

"Oh wow. I appreciate it, Aunt Della, but I can't tonight. Miss Edna invited me for dinner."

Della's eyebrows rose. "Edna Boyd? Well, I can't compete with her cooking. That woman puts her foot in everything she makes."

Ben laughed, "Yes, ma'am, she does."

Della studied him. "You doing okay, baby? You look tired."

"Just a long day."

She eyed him. "Well, you come by Sunday after church. I mean it. I'll make your favorite."

"Yes, ma'am."

She disappeared back inside, and Ben could hear pots clanging in the kitchen.

Ben moved toward the porch steps, then stopped. "Uncle Vern... when you came to talk to me after Daddy died. Did it help? Honestly?"

Vern considered the question. "Wasn't supposed to fix anything. Grief doesn't work that way. But I think..." He paused. "I think it helped you know you weren't alone." He met Ben's eyes. "That's all you can do for Theo's boy. Let him know he's not alone. You more than anyone understand how that boy feels."

Ben nodded.

"And Ben?" Vern stood slowly. "You did good, coming down here. Building something new. Your daddy would be proud of the man you've become. Badge or no badge."

The words hit harder than Ben expected. "Thanks, Uncle Vern."

The drive home didn't take long. He parked in the driveway and headed inside, stripping off his sweat-soaked shirt before he'd even reached the bathroom. The shower ran cool at first, thanks to the old water heater taking its time.

The cold water helped clear his head.

Uncle Vern's words kept circling back.

Ben dried off and pulled on a clean pair of jeans and a light blue henley. He grabbed his keys and wallet and locked the front door. The evening air had cooled slightly, the sky turning shades of pink and orange. Ben climbed into his truck and headed toward Sweetgrass.

He didn't know why, but Ben wondered if Kat would be at dinner tonight.

Chapter 7

Sweetgrass Bed and Breakfast
Friday, June 6 at 5:48 p.m.

The aroma of something rich and savory pulled Katrina from her room before she'd made the conscious decision to go downstairs. At some point, while staring at the ceiling, she'd taken another much needed nap. She looked at the time on her phone 5:48 p.m. That explained the delicious smells. Edna had mentioned dinner would be at 6:00 p.m. Just in time. Katrina headed to the bathroom to get ready.

She paused at the top of the stairs, hearing voices from below. One was a deeper voice. Male. Her first instinct was to retreat, but she was starving. Besides, it might be the young couple down the hall. Edna did say meals were included with the room. That would make sense.

Katrina continued down the stairs, announcing each step with a creak. When she finally reached the kitchen, she saw a man at the island, his back to her.

Edna spotted her in the doorway. “Come on in, honey. Dinner’s almost ready.”

The man turned. It was the landscaper guy. He’d changed since this morning, wearing a light blue henley that stretched across his broad shoulders and dark denim jeans. Their eyes met, and Katrina felt the same jolt she’d experienced twice before. She wasn’t afraid of him, but there was something about him.

The man possessed a rugged handsomeness; he seemed to hold his body with confidence, but not arrogance.

“Miss Kat.” He gave her a polite nod. “Good to see you again.”

“You too.” Her voice came out steadier than she expected.

A woman emerged from a room in the back of the kitchen Katrina hadn’t noticed earlier. It appeared to be a separate area of the house, and Katrina wondered if it might be where Edna and her family stayed. The younger woman, with her hair in long twists pulled back from her face, looked to be in her early thirties. Katrina recognized the family resemblance to Edna.

“You must be one of our new guests this weekend.” The woman’s smile was genuine. “I’m Tracey. Edna’s my aunt.”

“I’m Kat.” She returned the smile. “Nice to meet you.”

A boy of about six or seven burst into the kitchen from the side door wearing a Black Panther t-shirt paired with what looked like pajama shorts.

“Mama, is it time for dinner? I’m *starving*.”

"Jayden, manners." Tracey caught his shoulder, redirecting him toward Katrina. "Say hello to Miss Kat. She's staying in the Blue room."

The boy looked up at her with bright, curious eyes. "Hi, Miss Kat. Are you on vacation? We get lots of vacation people."

"Jayden." Tracey's voice held a warning.

"It's fine." Katrina gave Jayden a real smile. "I'm... taking a break. Getting some rest."

Jayden nodded. "That's what Mama says when she's tired of her computer."

Tracey set a basket of rolls on the table. "Aunt Edna, are the other guests joining us?"

"No, they headed out. Mr. Sanders already made a reservation for them. They are on their honeymoon, but we'll see them for breakfast in the morning." She turned to Katrina with a warm smile. "Have a seat, honey. Ben, you can sit across from Kat."

Katrina sat down, trying not to look at Ben as he pulled out the chair across from her.

Jayden sat in the chair next to Ben and Tracey sat next to Katrina.

Ben held up his fist, and Jayden gave him a fist bump.

"I'm glad you're eating with us, Mr. Ben. Mr. Emmett had to go out of town. So now I'm not the only guy." He turned to Katrina and faked whispered behind his hand, "Mr. Emmett is Mom's boyfriend. He's a lawyer." Jayden stopped talking long enough to take a swig of water from the table. He had to hold the glass with two hands. Once he placed the glass down, he started right back up again. "Miss Kat! Did you know Mr. Ben used to be a police officer? He caught bad guys!"

Katrina glanced at Ben, she noticed he went still.

Police.

"Jayden." Tracey's voice held a gentle warning. "That was a long time ago. Mr. Ben does landscaping now."

"But he *was* a detective," Jayden insisted. "Like on TV!"

"That's enough, baby." Edna's tone was kind but firm.

"It's okay." Ben took a sip of ice tea. His eyes landed on Katrina for a split second before he looked away.

Katrina felt more curious about the man in front of her.

Edna began bringing dishes to the table. Fried chicken, golden and crispy. Collard greens swimming in pot liquor. Macaroni and cheese with a browned, crusty top. The spread was enough to feed twice their number.

Katrina felt her eyes grow wide as she took in the feast.

Edna sat at the head of the table. "Grace first."

They all bowed their heads. Edna's voice rose, warm and steady: "Lord, we thank you for this food and for the company gathered at this table. Bless those who are hurting. Guide those who are lost. And remind us all that your mercies are new every morning. Amen."

"Amen," the others echoed.

Bless those who are hurting. Guide those who are lost.

Katrina's throat tightened. Those were words she needed to hear. She took small portions of each dish.

"So, Kat," Tracey said, passing her the macaroni. "Auntie mentioned you're from Atlanta?"

"Near there." Katrina kept her voice casual. "But my mother grew up in the Lowcountry. I used to visit when I was young."

"What part?" Ben asked.

She hesitated. "I'm not sure exactly. I was little. But I remember the water. The marshes."

He nodded slowly. "The Lowcountry has that effect on people. Gets in your blood."

"You're not from here originally?" The question slipped out before she could stop it.

His eyes twinkled as he grinned. "No. I'm from Atlanta. Born and raised. Moved here about three years ago."

"Small world," Katrina murmured.

Ben reached for a roll. "Small world, indeed."

Katrina directed her eyes back to her plate. Her stomach was doing cartwheels, and it wasn't because of the food. Ben had some mysteriousness behind those eyes. Despite her own circumstances, he intrigued her.

What was his story?

Katrina darted glances at Ben, while Jayden dominated the table with stories from camp. Tracey shared news about a new client, some bakery downtown that wanted a rebrand. From what Katrina could figure out, it sounded like Tracey worked for the Beaufort Chamber of Commerce.

"Speaking of work." Edna set down her fork. "Tourist season's about to hit, and I still haven't found anyone to help out around here."

Tracey sighed. "Auntie, we need to get someone soon. You can't keep running Sweetgrass by yourself. I was hoping we could find someone by Memorial Day for you."

Edna shook her head. "It's not like I didn't try. The last girl spent more time on her phone than working."

Ben spoke up. "What about posting on the community board at Second Baptist? Might find someone from the congregation."

"Good idea." Edna pursed her lips. "But with summer coming, most of the young people are already committed to other jobs."

Katrina's fork hovered over her plate. "What exactly would the job involve?"

Every head at the table turned toward her.

Katrina felt her cheeks grow warm. "I have some experience. I mean, making things look nice..." she trailed off, suddenly aware of how strange this must seem. A woman who'd arrived that morning now inquiring about work.

Edna's eyes studied Katrina carefully. "You said you weren't sure how long you'd be staying."

"I'm not." Katrina took a breath. "But I could use something to do while I figure things out. And if you need help," she shrugged, trying to appear more casual than she felt, "seems like it could work for both of us."

Tracey and Edna exchanged a look.

"Well," Edna dabbed at her mouth with her napkin. "I suppose we could do a trial run to see how things go. Let's talk more tomorrow."

Katrina nodded. She could feel Ben's eyes on her, but he didn't say anything.

After dinner, Katrina helped clear the table even though Edna protested she was a guest. Tracey took Jayden through the door that Katrina saw were the family quarters. Ben lingered in the kitchen, drying dishes as Edna washed them.

Katrina wasn't ready to go up to her room yet, so she explored the sitting room. When she'd arrived earlier, she'd been too tired to take in the decor. The big bay windows in the front grabbed her attention. The sun's slow descent altered the sky with orange and pink tones. Coupled with the azaleas outside the window, the vividness of the scene struck Katrina. It made her feel alive.

But then a memory sucked her back into the past when she stood at another window.

Atlanta, Georgia
Eight Months Ago

When Julian offered her a getaway at his lake house on Lake Lanier, she'd hesitated. Katrina had never gone anywhere with a man before, definitely not out of the city. But Julian had taken her platform to an entirely new level. She never thought she would expand her beauty platform to include an app. The commission alone had been more than she had made in six months.

Despite the money, she really had been enjoying using the LifeTrack app. She loved how the app integrated everything, including scheduling her social media posts, fitness tracking, her personal calendar, and even location-based recommendations. It felt natural to encourage her followers to download it.

What she hadn't expected was Julian's interest in her. He wasn't her type. But here they were, dating for two months. It was Katrina who insisted on keeping their relationship private. It was enough that she spent her time creating content and showing GRWM sessions every week. Get Ready With Me was one thing; her private life was off-limits.

That weekend, she insisted on driving her own car. Just in case. Julian fascinated her, but he also made her anxious. Sometimes his swagger and confidence could be overwhelming.

When Katrina arrived at the expensive lake house, she almost turned around and drove the hour back to Atlanta. Julian greeted her at the door and instructed a staff member to grab her luggage from her car. By the time Katrina finished touring the home with its modern furniture, high ceilings, and glass windows showcasing a private dock, she was shell-shocked. Julian was comfortable with his wealth.

After a nap, she stood on the back deck.

“You’re not posting the view?” Julian inquired as he joined her.

Katrina looked away from the dock, where she’d been taking in the pristine water. “I feel like all I do is create content for social media without experiencing life at all. I want to enjoy this view.”

“I like the sound of that.” He’d come up behind her, wrapped his arms around her waist. “You deserve this time. And you’re all mine.”

Mine.

The word had sent a small thrill through her then. Later the sponsorship. The app. Julian.

All of it became her nightmare.

Sweetgrass Bed and Breakfast
Friday, June 6 at 7:32 p.m.

Voices snapped her from the memory. Katrina's ears perked up. Even though she wasn't in the kitchen, she caught a fragment of a conversation between Edna and Ben. Katrina didn't mean to eavesdrop.

Edna said, "I hope staying busy today helped you get through the anniversary. I know it was a hard day for you."

Anniversary? A wedding anniversary?

Of course a man like Ben would have been married. But the way Edna talked, it sounded like this was a day of sadness for him. Feeling guilty for listening, she decided to get some fresh air. She had her own problems right now.

Outside, she settled in a rocking chair, letting it rock gently beneath her weight. The sun sank down into the tree line across the street. It was even more beautiful witnessing it out here than watching the sky through the window.

In Atlanta, Katrina had always been too busy. Filming content, editing videos, answering comments, and managing sponsorships, she lived her life through social media, putting herself out there for strangers.

Interesting how after her great escape last night, she ate with strangers tonight and felt right at home. She'd been drawn to Edna and Tracey's talk about hiring help.

What was she thinking? That she could stay here?

The screen door creaked behind her.

Katrina tensed, but she didn't turn around.

Somehow, she knew it was him.

Chapter 8

Sweetgrass Bed and Breakfast
Friday, June 6 at 7:45 p.m.

Ben hung the dish towel on a hook by the sink. When he turned, he could see inside the Boyd's residence on the other side of the kitchen. He'd been inside the family room a few times. The center of the family quarters contained the history of the Boyd's. Framed photographs covered the walls and the fireplace mantel, as well as the coffee and end tables. Ben admired how Edna, along with her sister-in-law, Tracey's mother, had turned the generational family home into a thriving business.

He could hear Jayden chattering with Tracey. The energetic boy was always full of questions and reminded Ben of Theo's boys.

Should he call Sarah tonight? Was he ready to talk to Tony?

Edna touched his arm, startling him. "You sure you're okay, Ben? I know today was hard."

He smiled. "I'm good. Thank you for dinner. As always, I appreciate you. I should head home. Another busy day tomorrow."

Edna waggled her finger at him as they headed down the hallway. "You should take Saturday off for yourself."

Ben grinned. "Oh, I am. Gives me some time to work on a personal project."

"That's good." She looked up and then grabbed Ben's arm before lowering her voice. "I see Kat's outside. I'm worried about her. What do you think could be going on?"

Ben's jaw tightened. "Well, the cop in me says she's running from something. But I'm just a civilian, so it's not my business."

Edna gave him a look. "Mmhmm. Well, it might be nice for her to have someone to talk to since both of you are from Atlanta."

He eyed her. "Alright. Goodnight, Ms. Edna."

She grinned back at him. "Goodnight, Ben. Drive safe."

He stepped outside, planning to give Kat a quick goodbye and head to his truck. But something made him pause. He could blame it on Ms. Edna, but the young woman had caught his attention since she stumbled into the bed-and-breakfast earlier today.

Kat sat in a rocking chair, looking out at the yard. Even though he knew she was a tall woman, somehow she looked small. Not fragile, but alone.

Keep walking, Ben.

But his feet didn't listen.

"Mind some company?"

She glanced at him before shrugging.

Ben leaned against the porch railing instead of sitting, giving her space. "Did you enjoy the meal?"

"I did. I think I ate enough for three people." Kat asked. "Does she always cook like that?"

He chuckled. "Ms. Edna doesn't know how to cook small. Says it's not worth dirtying the pans unless you're feeding a crowd."

A ghost of a smile crossed her face. He liked how it brightened her eyes though it was brief. They fell into silence, but it wasn't uncomfortable.

He used to be better at starting conversations with women. Why he'd gotten rusty since he moved here, he didn't know. Theo would have found it quite ironic.

Ben gave Kat a sidelong glance. She averted her eyes. Well, he still had something going on since he almost caught her looking at him.

"Are you really thinking about helping out around here? You just got here."

"I might." Kat paused. "I could use something to keep me busy."

"Staying busy helps," Ben said without thinking.

Kat looked at him then. Really looked.

She was stunning!

"Sounds like you know something about that."

He held her gaze. "Maybe I do."

The chair creaked as she set it to rocking with her long legs. "Jayden said you used to be a police officer."

"Yeah. Feels like a lifetime ago."

"What made you leave law enforcement?"

He grimaced. It was a fair question.

"Short answer. I lost someone." The words came out rougher than he intended. "After that, I couldn't do it anymore."

A car passed in front of the bed-and-breakfast, its headlights sweeping down the street before disappearing.

"I'm sorry," she said softly.

He cleared his throat. "It was three years ago. Today."

Her eyes widened. "And you worked all day and came to dinner? I would've been balled up in the bed somewhere."

Ben shrugged. "Ms. Edna doesn't take no for an answer. And..." He looked at her. "Being alone doesn't help."

Her eyes flitted away from his gaze.

Way to go, man!

He knew he should go, but he liked talking to her.

She didn't seem to mind his presence. "I'm such a city girl, all of this feels foreign and wonderful at the same time," she confessed in a breathless tone.

"That's the appeal of the Lowcountry" he said. "Quiet. Slow. The kind of place where nothing much happens."

"Is that why you came here?"

"Part of it." He paused. "My dad grew up here. Moved to Atlanta, met my mom. A lot of my other family members moved there as well. All but Uncle Vern. He's been here his whole life. After everything happened... I followed his advice. Unc was right. City life wasn't good for me anymore."

"Sounds like you made a good choice."

"I think so. I suppose if you decide to work for Ms. Edna, this place could be good for you too."

She didn't respond, but he saw her swallow hard.

He probably could have kept his advice to himself. Something told him she needed to hear it.

"I should head out." Ben took a step toward the porch stairs, then paused. "I hope you find what you're looking for here, Kat."

She stood and crossed her arms over her chest. "Thank you. For the company."

"Anytime."

Their eyes held for a moment again. Then he tipped his head in a nod and walked down the porch steps.

Ben climbed into his truck. Through the windshield, he could see her still standing on the porch, a silhouette against the warm glow of the windows. He turned the key, the engine rumbling to life. The headlights swept across the yard as he pulled away from the curb.

On the drive home, he couldn't shake the feeling that he needed to remain watchful about Kat. There was something there, not necessarily about her. He had good instincts about people. That's what made him a good detective for all those years.

She was scared of something, or someone. Maybe back in Atlanta?

He'd encouraged her to stay, but suppose trouble followed her here?

Chapter 9

Beaufort, South Carolina
Saturday, June 7 at 8:47 a.m.

She'd slept the whole night. Definitely a solid eight hours. Katrina lifted her head to stare at the photo of her parents on the nightstand. Her mother's smile. Her father's protective arm. Between the warm, soft bed, the tranquil room, and her beloved framed photo, Katrina felt a peace she hadn't experienced in months. No nightmares of Julian.

Thank you, Lord! Please continue to keep me safe.

With that short, whispered prayer, she sat up slowly. By the time her feet touched the rug by the bed, she was ready for the day. She had decisions to make. After a hot shower, she dressed in a t-shirt and jeans. Then she pulled a bag out of her suitcase. She needed to check to see if there was a safe in the room or on the premises.

In the meantime, she unzipped the bag to find all the cash she'd accumulated the last few weeks. She counted it out on the quilt. She'd paid Edna $360 for three nights. That left her with $2640. If she stayed here, she could do that for three weeks, but then she would have to tap into her other money. She wasn't ready to do that yet. It was imperative that she kept her electronic footprint nonexistent.

She wasn't safe yet.

Katrina tucked the money back into the bag and covered it up with her clothes inside the suitcase. Her stomach growled, ready for breakfast.

She took a deep breath before opening the bedroom door. The hallway was quiet, but she could hear voices downstairs. She descended the curved staircase slowly, her hand trailing along the smooth wooden banister. The aroma of coffee and something sweet grew stronger with each step.

When she reached the kitchen, she saw Edna at the stove, flipping what looked like French toast. The young couple sat at the small table near the window, their heads bent close together over a phone.

Edna turned and smiled. "Good morning, honey. Come on in. I hope you slept well."

"I did. Thank you." Katrina stepped into the kitchen, hyper-aware of the couple's eyes lifting to look at her. She'd been in her room most of yesterday, so she hadn't been very social.

The woman was beautiful with light brown skin, golden brown box braids pulled into a high ponytail. She wore a pale yellow sundress. The man beside her had deep brown skin, close-cropped hair, and black-framed glasses.

The woman grinned. “Hey, I’m Simone. This is my husband, Chase. We’re on our honeymoon.”

“Congratulations,” Katrina managed. “I’m Kat.”

“Nice to meet you,” Chase said with a grin.

“What’s on your agenda today?” Simone asked.

Kat shook her head. “Not sure yet.”

Edna set a plate of golden French toast in front of Katrina before she could respond. “Sit, honey. Coffee or tea?”

“Coffee, please.” Katrina slid into the empty chair across from the couple, grateful for the table between them.

“This place is gorgeous,” Simone said to Edna. “I’ve been posting photos all morning. My followers are going to lose their minds when they see this kitchen.”

Katrina’s hand froze halfway to her fork.

Followers. Posts. Please don’t take any photos of me!

She forced herself to pick up the fork and cut into the French toast.

Simone angled her phone toward Chase. “Babe, look at the engagement on the sunset photos from last night. Three hundred likes already.”

“That’s because you’re beautiful,” Chase said, kissing her temple.

Simone laughed and went back to scrolling. “Okay, I need to post this breakfast. Miss Edna, can I tag the B&B? Do you have an Instagram account?”

"Oh, honey, I'm not on the social media," Edna said with a wave of her hand. "But you're welcome to post whatever you like."

Katrina watched as Simone angled her phone to capture the perfect shot of the French toast. Then she snapped photos rapidly.

Katrina knew that rhythm and observed as Simone carefully selected a photo. Chase kept eating, more interested in his plate than the phone.

Katrina thought back to when she used to do the same thing. The careful composition. The hashtag strategy.

Julian had been taking his own photos.

"You okay?" Simone's voice pulled Katrina back to the present.

Katrina realized she'd been staring. "Sorry. Yeah, I'm fine. Just tired."

"I feel you," Simone said. "We didn't sleep much either." She exchanged a look with Chase that made him laugh.

Edna set a mug of coffee in front of Katrina. "How do you take it?"

"Black is fine."

The three of them ate in comfortable silence for a few minutes. The only sounds were Edna chopping veggies on the counter. Katrina wondered what the woman was planning for lunch. She hadn't seen a menu. Every meal had been a pleasant surprise.

"So what brings you to Beaufort?" Simone asked. "Vacation?"

Katrina swallowed a bite of French toast. "Something like that. My mother grew up in the Lowcountry. Thought I'd come see it for myself."

"That's sweet," Simone said. "Family roots are important."

Chase nodded. "My grandmother's from Gullah country. She used to tell us stories about growing up on the islands. I've been wanting to visit for years."

"Well, you picked the right time," Edna said. "Summer's just starting. The beaches are beautiful, and you won't find better seafood anywhere."

Simone's phone buzzed. She glanced at it and smiled. "My sister wants to know if we're having a good time. Should I tell her we're being fed like royalty?"

"You better," Chase said.

Katrina watched as Simone typed a response, then took a selfie with Chase, both of them grinning at the camera.

"Miss Edna, this was amazing," Chase said, pushing back from the table. "But we should get going if we want to make the most of the day."

"Y'all have a wonderful time," Edna said. "And if you need any recommendations for lunch or dinner, just ask."

Simone stood. "Thanks for breakfast, Miss Edna. It was perfect."

The couple headed upstairs to grab their things, leaving Katrina alone with Edna in the kitchen.

Edna refilled Katrina's coffee and settled into the chair Simone had vacated. "You sleep alright, honey?"

Katrina admitted. "Better than I have in a long time."

"Good. That's good." Edna sipped her own coffee. "I've got three more bookings for next week. Summer season's picking up. You ever work in hospitality, Kat?"

Katrina thought about her YouTube channels. "Yes." Managing a robust social media content schedule, responding to comments and DMs. Then there was listening to pitches and negotiating sponsorships. It was a different kind of hospitality.

Edna nodded slowly. "Well, if you're looking for work while you're in town, I could use some help around here. Nothing fancy. Just the basics."

"What would I be doing?"

Edna grinned, "Oh, a little bit of everything, honey. Help me serve breakfast, clean the rooms when guests check out, change the linens, keep the place looking nice. I'll teach you as we go. It will keep you busy. And you'll meet some interesting people. My guests come from all over the world!"

Katrina thought the work didn't sound bad. But would staying make it easier for Julian to find her? He could find her anywhere if he really wanted to. He had the money and the technology.

She needed to stay, at least for a few weeks. See if she could make it work.

"Now, about the Blue room," Edna said. "If you take the job, room and board would be part of your pay. You'd stay right where you are. I'll put new guests in the other rooms."

Katrina blinked. "Are you sure?"

"I think the Blue room has found the person who needs it most right now. I'd rather have reliable help than squeeze every dollar out of bookings. Two hundred a week cash, plus your meals and the room. Does that work for you?"

Two hundred dollars a week. Room and board included. That meant her savings could last months instead of weeks.

Katrina felt her throat tighten. "Why would you do this for me?"

Edna studied her for a long moment. "Because I've been running this place long enough to recognize when someone needs a safe place to land. And because I've been praying for help this summer. You showing up when you did? That's no coincidence, honey."

Before she could stop them, tears sprang to her eyes.

"Oh, honey." Edna reached across the table and touched her hand. "Whatever brought you here, the Lord will take care of it." She stood. "Now you paid for that room for three days. Go out and enjoy yourself. Get to know the town of Beaufort."

Katrina nodded. "I don't know how to thank you."

Edna winked. "You will."

Katrina slowly climbed the stairs to the Blue room. She walked inside, closed the door, and leaned up against it. This time, she didn't stop the tears from falling.

Thank you, Lord. Somebody is looking out for me.

She looked around the room. Ms. Edna was right. She needed to get out of this room and learn her surroundings.

Katrina grabbed her tote bag and car keys. Though she wasn't a fan of shopping in-person, a Walmart would have anything she needed. She missed the days of packages from sponsors and her own online shopping piling up at her front door. Now she would have to venture out into the wild.

The morning air was warm and heavy, carrying something sweet from the garden. Katrina climbed into the Honda, which still felt foreign to her. She backed out of the driveway and headed toward town, following the route she vaguely remembered from yesterday's exhausted arrival. The streets were busy for a Saturday morning in a small southern town. People walking dogs. Kids on bicycles. People who pointed and goggled like obvious tourists.

It didn't take long for her to find the Walmart and pull into the crowded parking lot. Through the windshield, she could see people going in and out. Suddenly, she felt clammy, like she couldn't catch her breath. Instead of turning off the engine, she cranked up the air conditioner and turned the vent toward her face.

You just need to get a few items, leave and get back to Sweetgrass.

As she gripped the steering wheel, a thought came to her. Katrina reached inside her tote bag and pulled out sunglasses and a hat. She felt silly putting them on like she was trying to disguise herself. These parking lots had cameras and… She was probably being paranoid. Still, the panic attack subsided after she placed the black baseball hat on her head. It fit nicely against her cropped hair.

She looked in the mirror. With the cap and sunglasses on, she barely recognized herself. Katrina grabbed her tote bag, locked the car, and headed inside. The automatic doors whooshed open, and cool air washed over her. She grabbed a basket and moved with as much purpose as she could muster.

Inside her head, she ticked off what she needed. Shampoo. Conditioner. Then a display of cheap t-shirts and leggings caught her eye. She removed her shades and stuffed them in her tote bag. After locating her size, she grabbed several different colors.

"Kat?"

Her blood went cold.

She turned slowly.

Ben stood at the end of the aisle.

Oh no! Why would she run into the only other person she knew in town?

Katrina's pulse hammered in her ears.

"Hey," he said, walking closer. "Didn't expect to run into you here."

She forced herself to smile. “Just picking up a few things.”

His gaze dropped to her basket. “You settling in alright at Miss Edna’s?”

“Yeah. She’s been really kind.”

“That’s good.” Ben gazed at her. “Looks like you’re planning to stay in Beaufort longer?”

She gulped, “I might be.”

He nodded slowly. “Well, if you need anything, I’m around. Been here only a few years now, but I know the area pretty well.”

“Thanks. I appreciate that.” Her eyes flicked to his basket. “What are you planning to do with that?”

Ben glanced down. “Working on a rocking chair at home. Just a hobby, really. My dad taught me woodworking when I was a kid.” He picked up one of the cans. “This is the finishing coat. Makes the grain pop.”

She smiled, and for just a moment, her shoulders relaxed slightly. “That must be nice. Making something with your hands.”

“Yeah. Keeps me busy.” He set the can back in the basket. “Better than sitting around thinking too much.”

Ben intrigued her. She wondered what he would be thinking about then caught herself from lingering any longer. “I should get to the checkout,” Katrina said, gesturing to her basket.

“Right. Yeah. Good seeing you.”

“You too.”

Katrina turned and headed for the checkout, forcing herself not to rush. To act normal. Like a person who wasn't running from anything.

But she could feel his eyes on her back as she walked away.

Calm down. He's not Julian.

Chapter 10

Beaufort, South Carolina
Saturday, June 7 at 7:15 a.m.

The smell of sawdust and wood filled Ben's garage workshop before the sun had fully risen. Two weeks ago, he'd selected pine boards with good grain and minimal knots from the lumberyard for his current project. His dad would've been proud. At least Ben liked to think so.

Growing up in Atlanta, his dad's workshop had looked a lot like this one with tools hanging on pegboards and sawdust coating every surface. They'd built a porch swing together when Ben was twelve. Took them three weekends. His dad had been patient, showing him how to cut the boards, how to fit the joints, and how to sand with the grain. When they'd hung it on the front porch, his mama had cried. Said it was the most beautiful thing she'd ever seen.

Ben smiled at that memory. It was a good one to have especially since he'd been up since six. Sleep hadn't come easy at all last night. The anniversary of Theo's death had passed, but the weight of it lingered. He enjoyed the landscaping, but being inside this workshop, leaning into the woodworking skills his father had instilled in him was better than any therapy session.

This wasn't Ben's first rocker. Two years ago, he'd surprised Edna with the two rocking chairs on her porch. The old ones had grown worn and wobbly, not fit for guests. This new project would be larger than his usual builds. A double rocker, wide enough for two people to sit side by side.

The idea came to him when Edna mentioned how many couples she was booking lately. Tracey had submitted the bed-and-breakfast to be featured in a bridal magazine. The magazine interviewed Edna and featured the Sweetgrass not only in the magazine but on social media. The double rocker would be perfect for couples.

Edna had become like a second mama to him. He wanted to pay her back for all her kindness in any way he could.

Ben stepped back and surveyed the chair. The sanding was done. All that was left was the finish. He walked over to the shelf where he kept his stains and oils, then frowned. He forgot he'd used the last of the golden oak stain on the Hendersons's bench two weeks ago.

He checked his watch. It was time for a break. He could run over to Walmart to grab some stain and be back in an hour. Not sure why, but he really wanted to finish the chair today. Probably because of all the ideas he'd sketched in his notebook last night. There were a lot more projects he wanted to pursue.

Guilt stabbed him. He'd done those sketches instead of calling back Theo's son. He felt like a coward.

Ben cleaned as much sawdust as he could from his hands and arms at the utility sink in the garage. The drive didn't take long. He'd learned the roads quickly when he first moved here, especially the roads he needed to avoid. Walmart sat off Robert Smalls Parkway, a massive beige building surrounded by a parking lot. Saturday morning always had a decent crowd. He often avoided being around too many people when he could. But today wasn't one of those days. He would have to suck it up.

He grabbed a handbasket and headed toward the hardware aisle in search of wood stains. To his dismay, there were three different brands of the golden oak. He picked up one, read the back. Checked the price. Set it down, picked up another. The Minwax was on sale. It was a good brand and he remembered his dad had used it. Grabbing two cans, he set off toward the front for the registers.

Along the way, he smiled and returned waves as he passed people he knew. Out the corner of his eye, a familiar figure caught his attention.

Ben stopped short.

The woman looked up.

"Kat?"

Her eyes went wide, just for a second, like a deer caught in headlights.

"Hey," he said, walking closer, hoping that his voice was casual. "Didn't expect to run into you here."

She gave him a small smile. "Just picking up a few things."

His gaze dropped to her cart. "You settling in alright at Miss Edna's?"

"Yeah. She's been really kind."

"That's good. She's good people." Ben gazed at her. "Looks like you're planning to stay in Beaufort longer."

She looked away, "I might be."

"Well, if you need anything, I'm around. Been here only a few years now, but I know the area pretty well." He wanted to kick himself.

Why did he say that?

"Thanks. I appreciate that." Her eyes flicked to his cart. "What are you planning to do with that?"

Ben glanced down at the wood stain. "Working on a rocking chair at home. Just a hobby, really. My dad taught me woodworking when I was a kid." He picked up one of the cans. "This is the finishing coat. Makes the grain pop."

For just a moment she appeared relaxed. "That's nice. Making something with your hands."

"Yeah. Keeps me busy." He set the can back in the cart. "Better than sitting around thinking too much."

Her shoulders seemed to tense again. The walls went back up.

What did he say wrong?

"I should get to the checkout," Kat said.

"Right. Yeah. Good seeing you."

"You too."

Ben watched her go, noting the way she glanced around the store as she headed toward the checkout. He hadn't missed the baseball hat on her head.

She was definitely hiding.

At the register, Ben loaded his items onto the belt while the cashier, a tired-looking woman in her fifties, scanned them. He paid with his debit card, grabbed his bags, and headed out to the parking lot.

Ben started the engine to cool off the truck. He'd walked away from his life in law enforcement, but he couldn't seem to shake the persistent sense that something was going on with Kat.

It wasn't his business. She was Edna's guest, and Edna was a better judge of character than most people he'd ever met. If Edna thought Kat was safe to have around, then she probably was.

And if Kat was running from someone, she probably needed to be left alone. She might need some healing like he did. The last thing she needed was a former detective in her business.

Was that what he was offering her back there inside Walmart?

Or was he just attracted to her and wanted to get to know her better? It had been a long time since he'd been around a woman.

Ben chuckled at himself as he pulled out of the parking lot to head back toward his house. Back in his garage, he unloaded the wood stain and set it on the workbench. After opening one of the stain cans and stirring it with a paint stick, the smell of wood oil filled the space. This was what he was supposed to be doing. Building things. Creating something good. Staying out of other people's problems.

Ben dipped a clean rag into the stain and began working it into the wood, following the grain. The motion was soothing. Wipe, blend, repeat. Watch the golden color bring out the beauty hidden in the pine.

Ben's phone buzzed on the workbench.

He almost ignored it. Saturday morning, he wasn't on call for any jobs. Probably spam. But when he glanced at the screen, his chest tightened.

Atlanta area code.

For a long moment, he just stared at it. Was it Sarah again?

Ben set down the rag and picked up the phone, thumb hovering over the answer button.

It buzzed again.

He answered. "Hello"

"Ben? It's Jenna."

His hand tightened on the phone.

Detective Jenna Cole. Atlanta PD. Cold Case Unit.

The woman he'd dated before everything fell apart. The woman who'd tried to be there for him after Theo died. The woman he'd pushed away along with everyone else.

He croaked her name. "Jenna?"

"Hey, Ben. I know yesterday was the anniversary," she said. "I wanted to check on you."

"I appreciate it."

Jenna paused. "Also, we're reopening Theo's shooting investigation. I wanted you to hear it from me."

Ben set down the phone, put it on speaker, and braced both hands on the workbench.

"You got a suspect?"

"Not yet. But we're closer than we've been since it happened. Someone from a more recent case could make the connection for us."

Ben couldn't stop himself drifting back to that night.

The car. The darkness.

Theo checking his gun.

Ben grabbed his arm. "We should wait for backup."

Theo spun on him. "We'll lose him. It's just surveillance. We're not going in."

Ben felt the adrenaline rise in chest. He didn't have a good feeling about this.

But Theo was his partner. The man always had good instincts.

"Ben? You still there?"

Jenna's voice pulled him back to the present.

The garage. The rocking chair. The wood stain on his fingers.

He responded weakly. “Yeah. I’m here.”

“Look, I know this is hard. And I debated calling you.” Jenna lowered her voice. “We haven’t forgotten him. Haven’t given up. I wanted you to know that.”

Ben stared at the grain of the pine wood in front of him, hoping it would ground him. “Thanks for telling me.”

Jenna remained silent for a beat. Then she asked, “How are you doing down there? That town is called Beaufort. Did I say that right?”

“Yeah, you got it.” He took a deep breath. “And I’m fine.”

“Really, Ben?”

“I’m good, Jenna. Really.” His voice came out rougher than he intended. “Just... keep me posted on the case.”

“I will. And Ben? For what it’s worth... it wasn’t your fault. It never was.”

She hung up before he could respond.

He picked up a fresh rag. Dipped it in the stain and went back to work applying the stain. Then he stopped. Ben closed his eyes, but that was a mistake. Memories flooded his mind, blocking out the smell of sawdust and wood stain, transporting him back to three years ago.

The gunshot cracked through the night, sharp and final.

Ben's training kicked in before conscious thought. He was moving, weapon drawn, rounding the corner toward the east side. His radio was in his hand.

"Shots fired! Officer needs help! Corner of Industrial and Fifth!"

He saw Theo on the ground before he reached him, one hand pressed against his chest, the other still gripping his weapon. Dark blood spreading across his shirt.

"No, no, no, no—" Ben dropped beside him, his hands replacing Theo's against the wound. Hot blood pulsed between his fingers. Too much blood. "Theo, stay with me. Stay with me, brother."

Theo's eyes were wide, confused. Surprised. His lips moved but no sound came out.

"Officer down! Officer down!" Ben shouted into his radio. "I need an ambulance at Industrial and Fifth! Gunshot wound to the chest! Officer down!"

"Ben—" Theo's voice was barely a whisper. "Sorry—"

"Don't you dare." Ben pressed harder, trying to stop the bleeding, trying to fix it, trying to hold his partner together through sheer force of will. "Don't you apologize. You're gonna be fine. Ambulance is coming. You're gonna be fine."

Theo's hand found Ben's wrist, grip weak. "Tell Sarah—tell her—"

"You tell her yourself. You're gonna be fine."

But Theo's eyes were already losing focus, his grip loosening.

The sirens were getting closer, but Ben knew they would be too late.

Theo's hand went slack.

His eyes snapped open. There was no way he was going to finish this chair today.

He couldn't. Not now.

Ben threw the cloth down on the floor. He leaned against the bench, forcing himself to breathe.

Jenna called with good news. He should feel hopeful, but his hands were shaking. All he felt was the familiar weight of guilt pressing down on his chest.

If only we had waited for backup, Theo would still be here.

Part Two

The Shift

Chapter 11

Two Weeks Later...
Beaufort, South Carolina
Friday, June 20 at 10:15 a.m.

Katrina sat in her car staring at the small house through the windshield. Her appointment with the real estate agent wasn't until ten-thirty. She'd been living in Beaufort for over two weeks now and even though Ms. Edna offered her room and board, Katrina was ready for her own place.

The Blue room was really the best room. During her time working at the bed-and-breakfast, she realized it had originally been a master bedroom, which accounted for why it had its own bathroom. The other rooms on the floor shared a luxurious, but communal, bathroom.

Her business sense just wouldn't let her allow Edna to continue her kindness. Katrina even thought about moving down the hall to the Yellow or Green room, but she'd grown used to having her own bathroom.

She needed her own place.

Just in case. The last thing she wanted to do was repay Edna's kindness with the kind of mess Julian could bring.

Three nights ago, she awoke from a nightmare. Julian had found her at Sweetgrass. He'd managed to worm his way inside and into her room. She'd woken up screaming and fighting. The sheets were twisted around her and she had been a sweaty mess.

Fortunately, the guests had checked out earlier that day and the rooms down the hall were empty. Still, she felt Edna's eyes on her the next morning at breakfast. Had her screams reached the family quarters? Neither Edna nor Tracey said a word.

Katrina had grown fond of both Edna and Tracey. The Boyd women were incredibly strong, having endured what they did when Tracey's father was wrongly incarcerated for murder. Tracey had shared with Katrina about moving away with her son to live in Florida.

It was Tracey who Katrina went to about the real estate agent. She felt like the single mom would understand the need for space and how to handle her Aunt Edna. During lunch in the kitchen three days ago, Tracey slid her laptop across the table.

"Use it whenever you need. I'm barely on it during work hours anyway."

The casual offer had made Katrina want to break down on the spot. After all the foolishness she'd endured from Julian, her winding up at the Sweetgrass had been a blessing. She'd spent that evening searching the local listings, realizing how much she missed her MacBook that she'd parted with before leaving Atlanta.

Here she was looking at the rental house she'd screenshot with her phone. Described as a cottage on the website, it sat back from the street, white with a blue front door and blue shutters. Katrina immediately fell in love with the small front porch. Flower beds lined the walkway. She was no gardener, but she remembered when her mom used to spend time outside on the weekends tending to flowers that looked a lot like these did.

Katrina had only lived in apartments. The last time she lived in a house was with her parents growing up. Now she imagined herself living inside this house. Maybe drinking her morning coffee on the porch. She longed to put roots down somewhere, anywhere that Julian couldn't find her.

I hope I'm making the right decision. I hope he's forgotten about me.

Katrina's grip tightened on the steering wheel. She couldn't think about him. Not when she was finally starting to feel like herself again.

Movement in her rearview mirror caught her attention. A silver Lexus pulled up behind her Honda and parked. Katrina watched as a cocoa brown woman stepped out wearing a navy and white dress that twirled around a slim figure. Her dark curls tumbled around her shoulders.

Katrina recognized Michelle Carver from the website. She grabbed her bag and climbed out of the car. The June heat wrapped around her immediately, thick and humid even at mid-morning.

"You must be Kat!" The woman approached, her hand extended. "I'm Michelle Carver."

Katrina shook her hand. "Nice to meet you, Ms. Carver."

"Please, call me Michelle." She pulled a set of keys from her black designer bag and gestured toward the cottage. "This just came on the market yesterday. You're actually my first showing."

Katrina experienced a flutter of excitement. She hadn't even walked in yet, but felt like claiming the rental.

Michelle unlocked the front door and pushed it open, stepping aside. "After you. Take your time, walk around, get a feel for it. I always tell my clients to trust their gut. You'll know within the first five minutes if a place is right."

Katrina stepped inside appreciating the cool air. The front door opened directly into the furnished living room. The hardwood floors and modern gray couches were a nice touch for the small space. Katrina immediately started thinking about adding a pop of color with accent pillows and throws. She liked how the morning light streamed in through the blinds.

"We just repainted a few weeks ago," Michelle said from behind her. "New ceiling fan too. The windows are original, but they're well-maintained. Double-paned, so they keep the heat out pretty well."

Katrina moved through the space, slowly taking it in. The living room flowed into a small dining area and then into the kitchen. Open floor concept like her old apartment.

She knew this was an older house, but someone had taken the time to modernize it. The kitchen had white cabinets with stainless steel appliances. There was plenty of counter space. And there was a window over the sink. She walked over to examine the view. Very pretty backyard and more flowers.

"I know it's not huge," Michelle said, "but it's efficient and cozy."

Katrina ran her hand along the countertop. She could see herself here making coffee in the morning or cooking dinner in the evenings.

"Two bedrooms down the hall," Michelle continued, leading the way.

The master bedroom was modest with a single window and a closet that was smaller than Katrina would have liked. But it would fit a queen bed and a dresser. That was enough.

The second bedroom was even smaller. "Could be an office," Michelle suggested. "Or a guest room. Lots of people use it for an exercise room."

Katrina nodded, but her mind was already spinning with possibilities. She could set up a small desk in here. She would need to buy a laptop, but that wasn't as important now.

"One bathroom between them," Michelle said, opening the door at the end of the hall.

Katrina peered inside. White subway tile on the walls, a vanity sink, and a claw-foot tub that had probably been there since the house was built.

"And here's my favorite part." Michelle walked back through the kitchen and opened a door Katrina hadn't noticed. It led to a back patio which opened out onto a well-maintained backyard bordered by a white privacy fence. A crepe myrtle tree bloomed in the far corner, its pink flowers bright against the green.

Katrina stepped on the patio. A whole yard to herself. Maybe she could get a dog. Or a cat.

"I can tell you like it." Michelle's voice was warm. "Trust me, I can always tell when someone sees themselves living somewhere. It's in the way you look at it."

Katrina saw herself here. A place to unpack completely and to rebuild the life Julian had destroyed. The thought of him sent a chill through her despite the June heat. She wished she could rid herself of him forever.

"Let's head back inside," Michelle said gently. "We can talk details."

They returned to the living room, and Michelle pulled a folder from her bag. "Okay, so here's what we're looking at. Rent is $850 a month. This includes utilities like electricity, water, and trash. Internet and cable, if you want those, you'd set that up yourself, but the whole area has good coverage."

$850. Katrina did the math quickly. Manageable, especially with what Edna was paying her.

"The owner prefers a one-year lease," Michelle continued, "but they might negotiate for the right tenant. And they're asking for the first and last month plus security deposit upfront."

Katrina's stomach tightened. $2550.

$3000 to move in.

She had the money sitting in a bank account under her real name. Over seventy thousand dollars, money she'd earned from sponsorships, affiliate links, and ad revenue. Money she'd been smart enough to save instead of spending on designer clothes and expensive trips like some influencers did.

But every time she thought about accessing it, her chest tightened with fear. Every withdrawal, every transfer, every time she accessed the account from a new location created an electronic trail. What if Julian had someone watching for any activity on her accounts? The paranoia was exhausting, but she knew he didn't mind engaging in illegal activities. He had the money and resources to do what he wanted.

"So," Michelle said, "what brings you to Beaufort? I understand you're working at Sweetgrass?"

"Yes. Just needed a change." Katrina kept her voice light. "Fresh start."

Michelle nodded like she'd heard that before. "The Low-country has that effect on people. Good place for new beginnings."

"I should mention," Michelle continued, flipping to another page in her folder, "a credit check and employment verification are required. Standard stuff."

Katrina's heart sank.

Credit check. Under what name? Kat Miles had no credit history. No employment history beyond two weeks at a bed-and-breakfast. Nothing.

"Is that going to be a problem?" Michelle's voice was gentle.

"I..." Katrina pulled out her phone. "I need to look at my finances."

"Listen," Michelle touched her arm. "If you're new to the area and worried about credit history, Edna Boyd's recommendation carries serious weight around here. Everyone knows Edna, and if she vouches for you, that matters."

A flicker of hope cut through the anxiety.

"And if you can pay a few months up front instead of just first and last," Michelle continued, "that shows financial stability with no need to dig into credit reports."

Katrina's mind raced. Three months up front for first, last, and the security deposit would be $2550. Another $850? $3400 hundred total. Four months would be $4250.

Doable. Scary, but doable.

"How many months would you recommend?" she asked.

"Three or four should do it. Especially with Edna's recommendation." Michelle smiled. "I've worked with nervous renters before. I get it. Sometimes you just need a little flexibility."

Katrina nodded slowly, not trusting herself to speak. Michelle wasn't pushing. Just offering solutions and, of course, probably trying to get a new tenant.

"Come on," Michelle stood and gestured toward the front door. "Let's step outside. I'll show you the neighborhood, and give you a better sense of the area."

Katrina was grateful for the fresh air when they walked out onto the front porch.

Michelle gestured up and down the street. "Quiet neighborhood. Mostly retirees and young families. Very safe and very low crime rate. The couple next door, the Hendersons, are lovely people. They've been here about fifteen years."

Katrina scanned the street. Neat houses with well-maintained yards. Mature trees providing shade. A couple of cars parked in driveways, but no one was outside. It felt peaceful. Nothing like the busy Midtown Atlanta street where she used to live, with its constant traffic and noise. This was the kind of place where you could disappear.

Then the deep rumble of a truck engine along with the metallic rattle of a trailer hitched behind it sliced through the quiet. She looked up just as a white Ford F-150 pulled into the driveway next door.

Hunter green lettering on the door: Wyatt Landscaping Services.

Her breath caught.

Ben.

He turned his head, and their eyes met.

Katrina felt frozen, caught between wanting to wave and wanting to run to her car.

"Oh!" Michelle's voice broke the spell. "Well, well. One of the perks of this neighborhood is the scenery."

Katrina tore her eyes away from Ben's truck. "What?"

Michelle was watching the F-150 with obvious appreciation. "That's Ben Wyatt. Does landscaping around here. One of Beaufort's most mysterious bachelors." She said it with the tone of someone who'd tried and failed to get information out of him.

Ben climbed out of the truck.

Katrina's heart fluttered in her chest.

He works next door? Of course he does!

She wasn't sure if that was comforting or terrifying. Maybe both.

Ben walked around the truck, dressed in dark jeans and a gray t-shirt. Katrina watched as he started unloading the lawn mower from the trailer. His muscles rippled through the t-shirt.

"So?" Michelle's voice pulled her attention back. "Should I draw up an application? I have a feeling this place won't last long on the market."

"I..." She swallowed. "I need to think about it. Can I let you know by Monday?"

Michelle's smile dimmed, but she nodded. "Of course. But I should mention I'm showing it to two other people this weekend. I'm not trying to pressure you, just want you to know the reality. Good rentals in safe neighborhoods go fast around here."

"I understand." Katrina felt a lump in her throat.

I really want this place. I need it!

Chapter 12

Beaufort, South Carolina
Friday, June 20 at 10:28 a.m.

Ben's hands gripped the steering wheel as he drove toward the Henderson's property, his mind still heavy from last night's phone call. He'd prayed about it and finally made the call. He didn't even know why he had stalled so long.

"*Uncle Ben?*" Tony's voice was deeper than he remembered, cracking slightly in that awkward fifteen-year-old way. "*Mom said you wanted to talk.*"

For a moment, Ben froze, unsure where to start. Then Uncle Vern's words came back to him: *Tell him about the man Theo was before that night. The partner. The friend.*

"*Yeah, I did. It's been awhile. How are you doing?*"

Ben's question was met with silence on the other end. Then Tony finally muttered, "*Okay.*"

"*You know, I really miss your dad. He had the worst jokes,*" Ben started, a smile tugging at his lips. "*And he'd tell them* during stakeouts, and I'd have to sit there pretending they were funny because he'd get so proud of himself."

A rumble came from Tony, that sounded a bit like a laugh. "Yeah? That sounds like dad."

"Like, we're sitting in a car at three in the morning, watching a warehouse, and he goes, 'Ben, why don't scientists trust atoms?' And I'm like, 'I don't know, Theo, why?' And he says—"

"Because they make up everything!" Tony finished, "He used to tell us that stupid joke all the time."

"He tell you the one about the restaurant on the moon?"

"Great food, no atmosphere."

"That's the one." Ben sighed. "My dad was killed when I was twelve too. They had to make me go to the funeral."

"For real. Why?"

Ben swallowed hard. "I didn't want to see him like that. He was my hero."

"That's how I saw my dad too."

The conversation flowed easier after that.

Ben said quietly. "Your dad was the best partner I ever had. Best friend too."

"Is that why you left? Stopped being a cop?" Tony asked.

"Yeah. I couldn't go back."

"Mom says you did everything you could. She doesn't blame you, Uncle Ben. None of us do. I hope we see you sometime."

They talked for a few more minutes after that, and when Ben finally hung up, he felt like he'd put down something heavy, something he'd been carrying for three years.

As he turned into the Henderson's driveway, Ben spotted a black Honda Civic and a silver Lexus parked in front of the rental property next door. Through his windshield, he could see two women on the front porch. Both women turned in his direction.

At first, he smiled when he noticed Kat. He hadn't seen her in a few days. Her hair had grown into a soft curly fro that framed her face.

Then he suppressed a groan when he saw Michelle Carver. The real estate agent had been trying to get his attention since he moved to Beaufort. She was attractive, but Ben had zero interest. Unfortunately, Michelle and her gossiping mother, Anita Carver, were good clients, so he had to wade the waters carefully.

Ben climbed out of the truck and strolled around to the front, his eyes locking with Kat's gaze. Something flickered across her face. He guessed maybe she didn't want anyone knowing she was looking at rental properties. It was a good sign that she wanted to put down roots here. Staying at Sweetgrass had its benefits, but he imagined she needed her own space.

Michelle waved, "Morning, Ben!"

Ben raised his hand in acknowledgment. "Morning, Ms. Carver."

Michelle stepped down from the porch and started in his direction. "How many times do I have to tell you? It's

Michelle." She stopped just a little too close, tilting her head up at him. "Glad to see you this morning. You working hard?"

He stepped back. "Yes, ma'am. "

She wrinkled her nose. "Ma'am. Really, Ben. We're the same age."

And how did she know how old he was?

Michelle turned and gestured toward Kat. "Ben, do you know Kat? She works at Sweetgrass."

Ben let his eyes roam over to where Kat had stepped off the porch. He liked the way the jeans fit on her. And there was an easiness to her shoulders that had gradually settled over the last few weeks. He couldn't help but grin.

"We know each other."

As she drew closer, Kat gave him a small smile. "Hey, Ben. Good to see you."

Michelle raised an eyebrow. "Oh, you two know each other."

He wanted to know her better. Okay. Why did that thought just crash into his mind?

Ben tore himself away from staring at Kat. He noticed a strange look on Michelle's face, like she tasted something sour. She looked at him and then began beaming at him with a wide smile before turning her attention to Kat.

"Ms. Miles, I will look to hear from you. Don't wait too long."

Kat nodded. "I promise I will call you on Monday."

"Perfect." Michelle spun around and placed her hand on his arm. "I'm still waiting on that dinner date."

Too stunned by her forwardness, Ben raised his eyebrow.

This woman doesn't quit.

She sashayed back to her Lexus, her heels clicking with each step. Ben watched her go, glad she was leaving. He wanted to talk to Kat.

"You and Ms. Carver a thing?" Kat asked, an amused look on her face.

"Absolutely not!" Ben wanted to make that clear. He gestured toward the house. "So," he said. "You're looking at the rental? Does Edna know?"

Kat cringed. "No."

Ben chuckled, "If you go with this place, it's a good, quiet neighborhood." He gave a head nod toward the house next door. "Mr. and Mrs. Henderson are good people. They've been here about fifteen years. The grandkids visit often."

A small smile tugged at Kat's lips. "You're selling this place harder than Ms. Carver."

He loved seeing her smile.

"Well, thanks to the real estate company Ms. Carver operates, I have steady work taking care of rentals like this one."

"Oh, so you would take care of the yard? That's awesome." A faraway look crossed her face as she looked back at the house.

She really liked the place.

"You seem interested."

Kat laughed. "Am I that obvious?" She sighed. "Edna's been so generous, but she could make money booking the room I'm occupying."

"No need to explain. If you take the place, welcome to the neighborhood."

"We'll see. I should let you get to work," Kat said.

He nodded. "Good to catch up with you."

She started to walk off, but turned around. "Can I ask you a question?"

He tilted his head, noticing the serious look in her eyes. "Of course."

Kat asked, "Do you know how far Charleston is from Beaufort?"

Surprised by her question, Ben thought about the times he'd driven to Charleston. "It's about an hour and a half, give or take. Traffic around Charleston can add time."

She looked like she was thinking hard about something. "What about Savannah?"

He raised an eyebrow. "Are you planning on leaving Beaufort, or is this some type of road trip?"

The nervous look she had when she arrived in town a few weeks ago returned. Not looking at him, Kat responded, "Just a road trip."

Ben wanted to ask her for more details, but answered her question. "Forty-five minutes, maybe an hour. It's closer than Charleston."

"Thank you, Ben."

"Anytime."

Ben needed to get started on the Henderson's lawn, but Kat's questions bothered him. Before she reached her car, Ben called out, "Kat?"

She turned back.

He walked over toward her and stopped, keeping some distance.

"If you need help..."

Kat's eyes widened. "I'm fine. Really."

He didn't believe her. She'd been hiding something since the day she arrived. He was assuming she was running from a situation. The victim and not the problem. While he'd been away from law enforcement for three years now, his instincts hadn't gone rusty.

"Look, I don't know what's going on, and you don't have to tell me." He kept his voice even. "But I was a detective in Atlanta for eight years. If you're in some kind of trouble, I know people who can help."

She looked away. "I appreciate that, but there's nothing—"

"I'm not asking you to explain." Ben stepped closer. "Just want you to know the option's there. That's all."

She eyed him, fear in her eyes. "Why would you think I need help?"

"Because Charleston and Savannah aren't road trip questions. They're how-far-can-I-get questions."

Kat twisted her hands. For a moment, she looked like she might say something else. She glanced up at him. "I'm not leaving town. But I need to take care of something. That's all."

"Okay." He held up his hands, backing off. "You know where to find me if you need help."

She nodded and moved quickly around the car to the driver's side.

Ben turned away and headed back toward the lawn mower. He glanced over his shoulder as Kat drove away.

He really needed to mind his business. But from the moment he saw Kat walk through Sweetgrass's door, her presence tugged at his need to protect.

Chapter 13

Beaufort to Savannah, Georgia
Saturday, June 21 at 9:15 a.m.

Katrina gripped the steering wheel as she merged onto Highway 170 heading west toward I-95. Katrina felt grateful for the peaceful transition from her stressed-out life in Atlanta. She'd been in Beaufort for over two weeks with no issues, but that anxiety crept back in the farther she drove away from Sweetgrass. It didn't help that Ben's words from yesterday still echoed in her mind.

If you're in some kind of trouble...

His curiosity shouldn't have surprised her. The man had been in law enforcement. For a brief moment, she wanted to spill everything to him. She didn't know why. Maybe it was the way he looked at her like he knew.

But that was crazy. He didn't know what she'd been through.

Could people tell she was scared by looking at her? Probably. Katrina glimpsed the fear in her eyes every time she looked in a mirror. Even now, as she peered up in the car's rearview mirror, fear was present.

Though she'd felt a glimmer of peace at Sweetgrass, her anxious thoughts were always at the edge of her mind. She often wondered if a guest would recognize her on the days she manned the check-in. And everyone was always snapping pictures on their phones. The other day she'd almost photobombed a couple taking a photo on the stairway. She'd jumped back out of the photo in the nick of time. The last thing she needed was for her face to show up online.

Maybe she was being a little silly, but she'd lived her life online. It could be a bit forward of her to think she'd been some type of celebrity, recognizable by anybody. She was just an influencer. But she couldn't give Julian any breadcrumbs.

He was a tech guru; he had some of the best programmers in the world working for him.

She hoped Julian would forget all about her. But he wouldn't. Because she knew what he'd been doing with his app.

What he'd been doing to me.

Atlanta, Georgia

Four Months Ago

“There you are.”

Katrina whipped her head up from her laptop surprised to hear *his* voice. She removed her headphones. “Julian?”

Katrina caught glances of people looking in their direction. She had purposely blended in with the crowd, wearing a T-shirt and sweats. Her locs were pulled back.

Julian donned a two piece suit, his dark blond hair perfect. This didn’t seem like a place he’d visit. She’d learned he preferred country clubs. It was how he grew up, being raised by wealthy parents. His family was well-connected allowing him to attend the best schools and, later, enter the business world with his first startup at age eighteen.

What was so important that he had to track her down? And then to track her down here. They’d never even been to this coffee shop together.

He’d leaned down to kiss her cheek before sitting across from her in the booth. “You didn’t answer my text or calls. You had me worried.”

She’d gestured at her screen, where she had CapCut open for editing. Katrina had shot enough content to create five reels. “I’ve been deep in editing. You know how I get.”

Julian didn’t even look at the laptop. “Don’t you have notifications turned on? What if I needed to reach you for something important?”

Like what?

But she kept her questions to herself. She'd been doing that a lot lately. Even questioning why she had gotten so involved with Julian. With all her other sponsorship deals, she'd kept to business. But she managed to get swept up by this man.

She tried to soothe him with a smile. "I'm sorry. I expected you to be busy all day."

"Well, I wanted to hear your voice. I called twice." He smiled but it didn't reach his eyes. "Where's your phone?"

For a brief instance, Katrina felt annoyed. Julian was interrupting her editing time. She hadn't posted anything on her socials in three days. That was too long for her. The reason she was here was to get out of her apartment. She spent too much time there with all her lights and camera.

It felt good to be around people.

She sighed and pulled her phone from her bag. Seeing his missed calls and the three texts, she felt a little guilty. "Sorry. I had it on silent so I can edit in peace." Then something occurred to her and she looked at him. "How did you find me here?"

Julian's green eyes sparkled like emeralds. "That's the whole point of LifeTrack. So the people who care about you know you're safe."

This wasn't the first time he'd brought up the LifeTrack app. He joked it was his baby. Katrina went above and beyond promoting and recommending the app to her followers. She had been one of the first major influencers pushing the app and she genuinely loved using it. The interface was intuitive, making organizing her life easy.

Something chilled her. She looked away from Julian and stared at her phone before tapping the settings.

Julian leaned in. “What are you doing?”

Quickly, she confirmed she didn’t have location sharing on. “Julian, I’m not sharing my location with anyone.”

She was cautious about not doing that on her socials.

Julian sat back and shrugged. “The app has other features. Background location for safety check-ins, arrival notifications—”

“But those only work if I share my location. Right?” Her editing long forgotten. “So, how did you find me?”

Something flickered across his face. Disappointment? Irritation? It was gone too quickly to read. “You’re overthinking this. I just wanted to know if you were okay.” He leaned forward, his green eyes intense. “You’re one of LifeTrack’s biggest advocates. Your followers trust your recommendations. If you’re not using the app the way it’s designed, how can you authentically promote it?”

She wasn’t sure it was fair for him to point that out, but Katrina dropped her concerns. It was because of the sponsorship with LifeTrack that she’d been able to boost her savings account, securing her future.

Later, she would realize she’d been right to question how Julian had tracked her down that day.

Near Savannah, Georgia
Saturday, June 21 at 10:03 a.m.

A semitruck roared past in the left lane, shaking the car. Katrina gripped the steering wheel tightly as her heart thumped in her chest. She couldn't think about Julian right now. Her mind needed to be on the road and on her mission.

Stick to the plan so he can't find you.

Katrina picked up the car's speed on I-95 South. Her goal was to do anything she needed to do online in Savannah. If Julian could track her, it would look as if she was still in Georgia, accessing her bank account in Savannah. It all felt so elaborate, like she'd been dropped inside some espionage movie, but she wasn't the spy.

Julian had been the one who'd infiltrated her life. Her privacy. She had to protect herself and stay ahead of him this time.

Katrina had only been to Savannah a handful of times, for brand partnership events. She liked the city and looked forward to being back, though she wouldn't have time to sightsee on this trip. Her goal was to be back at the Sweetgrass by early evening.

She appreciated Edna letting her take the day off. The woman had been a godsend. The room. The food.

Lord, that woman could cook!

In the past two weeks, Katrina was sure she'd put back on the weight she'd lost from stress, eating out of Edna's kitchen two to three times a day. Clothes that were hanging off her, weeks ago, now fit like they were supposed to.

And Katrina genuinely enjoyed working at the bed-and-breakfast. It brought her peace and gave her time to think.

The Savannah exit appeared on the green highway sign displaying three miles.She had made good time this morning. She took the exit, following the signs toward downtown. The city unfolded around her as she drove down the historic district. It shared some similarities to Beaufort, with its own massive, moss-draped oak trees.

The first thing she needed was Wi-Fi and privacy. Thankfully, Katrina had invested in a premium prepaid phone with a data plan. It looked like a smartphone and could connect to Wi-Fi and download apps. She missed her MacBook and iPhone but could do what she needed to do on this burner phone.

She used the phone's data to search for a nearby library branch. Logging into anything sensitive from her own IP felt like leaving a trail and a public computer was safer. She found the Bull Street Library and made her way there.

After pulling into the parking lot, she sat for a moment and scanned the area. A young woman with two kids was coming out of the library. Both kids had stacks of books in their arms. Reminiscent of Saturday mornings with her mom at the library, seeing them made Katrina smile.

Katrina grabbed her bag, locked the car, and headed inside. The library's air conditioning was a relief from the humid heat outside. She found a corner table away from the main desk, positioned so she could see the entrance. Ensuring there was no one around her, she logged into her bank account first. Then she focused on the numbers on the tiny screen.

Nearly seventy thousand dollars.

Katrina was thankful she'd put away thirty percent of everything she earned. With an accountant as a dad, she'd learned to be money savvy early. She'd worked hard for her money. Years and years of content creation, editing, engaging with followers, and building a brand. And she'd walked away from it all. Julian got to build his tech company, and she had to tear her small world down to get away from him.

She took a shaky breath and pulled out her notebook where she was keeping up with her budget. To secure the rental house and keep Michelle from digging into her credit history, Katrina would need a deposit plus four months of rent. Michelle had quoted $850 a month. That meant $4,250 upfront.

Katrina didn't want to touch the cash flow she had hidden at the Sweetgrass. She would have to withdraw that amount and more for other items. She would definitely need a bed and dresser to start.

After a quick search, Katrina discovered Truist Bank wasn't too far from the library. She headed out to her car and arrived at the bank within ten minutes. The humid heat made her shirt stick to her back. She pushed through the glass doors into the blessed cool of the bank lobby.

A cheerful brunette with large, framed glasses greeted her from behind the counter. "Good afternoon! How can I help you today?"

Katrina smiled. "First, I need a cashier's check, please."

"Absolutely. I'll just need to see your ID and get some information."

Katrina reached inside her purse. She'd been Kat Miles for the past two weeks, but today she had to be Katrina Noelle Bowen. She handed over her Real ID.

The teller took it with a smile. "And how much will the check be for?"

"4,250."

"Perfect. And who should I make it out to?"

"Carver Realty and Property Management."

The teller's fingers flew across her keyboard. "Okay, Ms. Bowen, I'll need you to sign here and here."

Katrina signed her legal name twice, the pen feeling heavy in her hand. Every signature was evidence. Every transaction, a breadcrumb. But what choice did she have?

"And will you be needing anything else today?"

Katrina hesitated. "Yes. I'd also like to withdraw some cash. Two thousand dollars."

"Of course. Let me get that for you."

Five minutes later, she walked out of the bank with a cashier's check folded carefully in her purse and two thousand dollars in hundreds tucked into her wallet. Despite the anxiety of the trail she'd established, she was excited about calling Michelle on Monday.

Famished, Katrina headed over to Panera Bread and ordered a Fuji Apple Chicken salad. She found a corner booth for privacy. While here in Savannah, she needed to make a call. She pulled out the second burner phone from her bag and dialed her aunt's number. The phone rang once. Twice.

"Kat?" Her aunt's voice was breathless, urgent.

"Hey, Auntie." Katrina's throat tightened. "I'm sorry I haven't called sooner."

"It's good to hear your voice. Baby, are you okay? Where are you?"

"I'm safe. I can't tell you where, but I'm safe."

"Kat, I've been so worried. People keep asking about you."

Katrina's stomach dropped. "What people?"

"You know I'm not on social media other than Facebook. Remember when I joined that Atlanta beauty Facebook group you created. There are women speculating about what happened to you. They're saying @KatsGlowUp just vanished overnight. No goodbye post, nothing."

Katrina closed her eyes. That was to be expected. She'd gone dark without explanation, Just deactivated everything, and made it all disappear.

"Kat—"

Something in her aunt's voice made her body still. There was such a long pause that Katrina called out, "Auntie, are you still there?"

"Yes, I wanted to tell you I'm glad you left town."

Katrina's pulse picked up. "What happened?"

"That man has been back here. He drove up in this big black SUV, but he wasn't driving. Some big man was the driver. Julian stepped out of the SUV like he thought he was somebody special. Rang the doorbell a few times. But I didn't answer. I stood, watched him on the camera and waited for him to leave."

Ice flooded Katrina's veins. Julian had been at Aunt Lola's house again.

Aunt Lola continued. "He freaked me out, Kat. That man leaned in and looked at the camera. Then he smiled."

Katrina sucked in a breath. Julian had done that to her before, showing up at her apartment.

I know you're in there, Katrina. You can't hide from me.

The memory made Katrina shake. She looked around the restaurant, noticing it had filled up. She leaned over, holding the phone closer to her mouth. "I'm sorry. I'm so sorry. This is my fault. I should never have stayed with you."

Aunt Lola answered sharply. "Don't you dare apologize for reaching out to family. I just wish I knew what he did to you. Why can't we go to the police?"

Because there was nothing she could prove. That was the problem. He'd gaslit her, tried to convince her that she was paranoid. That he hadn't been tracking her, just looking out for her. Julian was rich beyond words. And he had clout in the industry. Probably high-priced lawyers.

Who would believe her?

But he couldn't be harassing her aunt. Katrina swallowed. "Auntie, if he comes back, call the police."

Her aunt's voice came out low and fierce. "Don't worry. I will. And I might give him a piece of my mind. You just stay safe. Promise me!"

Katrina licked her lips. Her throat felt hoarse. "I promise. Please don't talk to him. I'll be in touch again soon."

Katrina clicked the phone off and stared down at the salad she hadn't even touched.

Had she put her aunt in danger?

Suddenly, she thought about Ben's offer yesterday.

I know people who can help.

Katrina realized she couldn't just hide from the world. Julian seemed determined to find her. He was obviously trying to find out where she was hiding. She needed to figure out a way to not have to keep looking over her shoulders.

Julian, you're doing too much!

Chapter 14

Beaufort, South Carolina
Saturday, June 21 at 5:15 p.m.

Ben pulled his truck into Sweetgrass's driveway, the rocking chair secured in the bed. The double rocker had taken him three weeks to complete. He climbed out of the truck and lowered the tailgate. The chair was heavier than he remembered, solid and substantial. He maneuvered it carefully out of the bed, his muscles straining as he carried it up the porch steps. He set it down near the railing, testing it to make sure it was sturdy. The chair rocked smoothly.

The screen door creaked open behind him.

"Benjamin Wyatt, what in the world—"

Ben turned to find Edna standing in the doorway, one hand pressed to her chest, her eyes wide.

He grinned. "Thought your guests might like it."

Edna stepped out onto the porch, moving slowly toward the chair. She ran her hand along the wood, stained to withstand the weather. "This is beautiful."

Ben lifted his baseball cap off his forehead. “I can paint it blue like the other two if you want.”

“Absolutely not. I love the stain. It brings out the wood grain.” Edna sat down in the new chair, settling into it with a small sigh. She rocked gently as a smile spread across her face. “It’s beautiful, Ben. Just beautiful.” She looked up at him, her eyes shining. “Thank you.”

“You’re welcome.”

“You’re staying for dinner,” she stood. “And I won’t take no for an answer. Tracey and Jayden will be here soon. I made pot roast.”

Ben opened his mouth to decline, but Edna was already heading inside, holding the screen door open for him to follow. He knew good and well he wasn’t turning down a meal from Edna.

The kitchen smelled like heaven as usual. He caught sight of fresh cornbread cooling on the counter. Ben settled at the table while Edna moved behind the island toward the stove where a big pot sat.

“The double rocker was really thoughtful of you,” Edna said, pulling plates from the cabinet. “That chair is going to get a lot of use.”

“I’m glad you like it.” He looked around. “Where’s Kat this evening?”

Edna raised an eyebrow. “She left early this morning for Savannah. Didn’t say much about it. Just that she had something to take care of.”

Ben shrugged. “Maybe she had errands.”

“Maybe.” Edna sat a pitcher of tea on the table. “I’m worried she might leave for good.”

That’s not what he saw yesterday. He frowned. “Why do you think that?”

“The way she looked this morning. Well, to be honest, she always looks like she’s carrying something heavy on her shoulders.” Edna pulled out a chair and sat. “That girl’s in trouble, Ben. I can see it in her eyes.”

Ben knew he should stay out of this, but Edna’s words echoed his own thoughts.

He sighed, “I don’t even know if I should mention this to you, but I ran into her yesterday at the house next to the Hendersons. Michelle Carver was showing Kat one of her rentals.”

Edna’s eyebrows rose. “She was looking at rentals?”

“Seemed genuinely interested.” He met Edna’s gaze. “I don’t think she’s planning to bolt. At least not yet.”

Edna’s shoulders dropped, and she leaned back against the chair. “That’s good to hear. I thought maybe... Well, I’m glad to be wrong.”

Ben looked at her, knowing he was diving in now. “Have you noticed something about her to give you the impression that she’s in trouble?”

“Tracey and I have noticed some things.” Edna laid her hands on the table. “Kat doesn’t have her own laptop or a real phone. I've seen her using one of those burner phones." She paused. "Aren't those for criminals?"

Ben tilted his head. "Not necessarily. People used them to stay off the grid."

Edna crossed her arms. "Off the grid from what?"

"From being tracked. Everything's electronic these days. GPS, social media, credit cards, email. Someone with a smartphone is basically sharing their location. It sounds like Kat's being careful."

Edna's eyes widened. "Who is she hiding from?"

"I don't know for certain." Ben hesitated. "But I've been thinking about it. More than I should."

"And?"

"My guess? She's running from a boyfriend. Maybe an ex."

Edna's hand went to her chest. "You think someone hurt her?"

"I've seen this before on the job back when I worked on domestic cases. Someone may have scared her enough to make her disappear." Ben thought about Kat's body language. "At first, she was more skittish around me than around you or Tracey. I'd have to consider it might be the reason why she's more hesitant around men."

Edna was quiet for a long moment. "Can you help her, Ben?"

"Miss Edna, I'm not a cop anymore—"

"I'm not asking you to be a cop." She leaned in toward him, her eyes direct. "I'm asking you to be a good man. Which you are, Ben Wyatt."

"I failed Theo," he said quietly. "What makes you think I can help her?"

"You didn't fail Theo. What happened to him wasn't your fault." She pointed a finger at him. "That girl needs to know someone who knows how to help."

Every instinct told him to refuse and not get involved. But he'd already been curious and had even offered his help yesterday.

"I can't promise anything."

"I'm not asking for promises. Just... keep your eyes open. Be there if she needs you."

Before Ben could respond, Tracey appeared in the doorway with Jayden bouncing beside her. "Hey, Aunt Edna. Ben." She smiled. "Something smells amazing."

"Pot roast. You're just in time." Edna gestured to the table. "Sit down, both of you."

Jayden scrambled onto his usual chair. "Mr. Ben! Did you see the new rocking chair on the porch? It's huge!"

"I made it," Ben said.

Jayden's eyes widened. "Really? That's so cool! How did you do it?"

"Jayden." Tracey put a hand on her son's head. "Don't pester Mr. Ben."

"It's fine," Ben said. "If it's okay with your mom, I can show you some basics sometime."

"Mom, can I?" Jayden beamed. "I want to make a car."

Ben chuckled. "That would be a challenge, but we might can do that."

They settled into dinner with the conversation flowing around Ben while he pondered Edna's request that he reach out to Kat. She almost said something yesterday, but quickly changed her mind.

She doesn't trust me yet.

After they'd eaten, Tracey told Jayden. "You can play a game before you get your bath tonight, since it's Saturday."

"Woo-hoo!" Jayden ran out of the kitchen toward the family quarters.

Edna started to clear off the table, but Tracey shooed her. "I got this." Tracey stacked the plates. "You need to stay off your feet for a while."

Ben stood and grabbed the glasses.

Edna fussed. "Ben, you don't need to do that."

He smiled. "My mama would disagree with you. She raised me to do my part."

Edna laughed. "Okay."

As Tracey stacked the dishes in the dishwasher, she asked. "Aunt Edna, have you heard from Kat yet? I thought she left for Savannah early."

Edna's face fell, and she looked over at Ben. "No, I haven't. Tracey, do you know why she went to Savannah? Does she have relatives there?"

Tracey shook her head. "She didn't mention it. I thought maybe she had some errands."

Edna frowned. "Maybe she's shopping. Did she accept the rental?"

Tracey gasped. "You know about that?"

Edna raised an eyebrow. "Thanks to Ben, I do. I was thinking the girl was going to leave us."

Ben blew out a breath. Leave it to him to let the cat out of the bag. He hoped Kat wouldn't be upset. "From what I understand, she was going to let Michelle know on Monday."

Edna clasped her hands together. "Oh, so she didn't confirm she wanted the rental yet. Well, suppose she went to look for places in Savannah. I really do like the girl being around. And what we talked about, Ben..."

Tracey looked from her aunt to Ben. "What were y'all talking about?"

"About Kat being in trouble. You know... the off the grid thing?"

Ben glanced over at Tracey to see if this was what she'd gathered.

Tracey nodded. "Yeah. I agree. She doesn't have a real phone. Like, who her age doesn't have an iPhone or an Android? She doesn't talk on the phone, no texting, and she's definitely not on social media. I can't recall a time where I didn't have my phone on me." Tracey reached in her jean's back pocket and pulled out her iPhone. "These devices are almost attached to our hands. And she only has those two suitcases. Really nice clothes, expensive name brands."

That was interesting. "So she has money?"

Tracey shrugged. "I just noticed that she has really nice things. Just not that many of them. Like maybe she packed her favorites."

Edna twisted her hands. "Well, I pray she comes back here safe. I don't get in people's business, but I know that girl needs help. I knew it the moment she showed up at the door a few weeks ago."

Ben really hoped Edna's theory about Kat looking for a place in Savannah wasn't true. But it could be perfectly logical. Someone on the run wouldn't stay in the same place long.

He turned to Edna. "I should head home. It's family time for y'all."

"You don't have to rush off," Edna said. The front door chimed. "Oh, that might be Kat." Edna hurried out of the kitchen.

Ben glanced at Tracey and then followed behind Edna. If Kat was just returning early evening, that meant she stayed most of the day in Savannah.

What had she been doing?

Edna opened the door, and Ben stepped back. It felt like déjà vu.

Like the day Kat had arrived.

Except this time when Kat stepped through the door, while she appeared exhausted, their eyes met. Though she didn't say a word, Ben decided, against his better judgment, he would stay.

Something has happened.

Chapter 15

Beaufort, South Carolina
Saturday, June 21 at 7:32 p.m.

Katrina stood in the doorway, every muscle in her body ached from the drive. She worried the whole way about her aunt. What had she done bringing Julian into not only her life, but her closest relative's life? The first person she saw after Edna opened the door was Ben. He looked like he was on his way out. His presence reminded her of the day she'd arrived.

Edna stepped aside. "Come in, honey. Have you eaten? I've got plenty of pot roast left."

Katrina's stomach had been in knots since the phone call with her aunt. She'd barely eaten the salad she'd bought at Panera Bread earlier, so she was ravenous.

Katrina followed Edna into the kitchen, hyperaware of Ben trailing behind them. After their conversation yesterday, she wondered if he had questions for her.

The kitchen was warm, filled with the lingering scents of dinner. Tracey sat at the table, and her face lit up when she saw Katrina.

"Kat! We were starting to worry."

"Oh, I'm sorry. I didn't mean to worry anyone." Katrina slid into a chair, her knees and backed ached even though she hadn't taken a long drive.

Edna fixed a plate and set it in front of her. Steam rose from the plate of carrots, potatoes, and chunks of roast over white rice. Edna cut a generous piece of cornbread and added a small slice of butter on top. Tracey poured sweet tea without asking. Ben took the seat across from her, giving her a small nod.

Katrina could sense the worry rolling off everyone at the table. These people had only known her for a few weeks, and their care surprised her. Once again she was grateful to God for guiding her to the Sweetgrass. She picked up her fork and took a bite of pot roast. The delicious warmth calmed her.

"Did you get everything done in Savannah that you needed to, honey?" Edna asked.

Katrina nodded. "Yes, ma'am. Just some business I needed to handle."

"That's a lot of driving for one day," Tracey said. "You must be exhausted."

"I am." Katrina took a sip of ice tea.

Edna sat down across from her, settling in. Her eyes were warm but probing. "Everything alright? You look troubled."

This was it. The moment to either keep lying or tell some version of the truth.

Katrina set down her fork and took a breath. "I wanted to let you know that I'd like to keep working here at Sweetgrass."

Edna's face lit up. "Oh! Honey, that's wonderful!"

"But I think it's time I gave you back the Blue room. You could book it." Katrina rushed on before she lost her nerve. "I'm going to call Michelle Carver Monday morning about the rental house on Ribaut Road."

"So you're staying in Beaufort?" Edna clasped her hands to her chest. "Girl, you had me worried. I thought you were moving on to Savannah."

Katrina smiled, the first all day. "No, I like Beaufort just fine."

Edna's face changed with concern. "Now, does the place come furnished?"

"It has some basics. There's a couch in the living room. Kitchen has all the appliances, very modern. I'll need bedroom furniture, kitchen supplies, things like that."

"We have so much stuff in storage!" Tracey jumped in. "Aunt Edna, what about that guest room furniture from when we remodeled?"

"Yes! And I've got extra dishes, linens, pots and pans..." Edna lifted her arms. "We can get you set up, no problem."

Katrina felt overwhelmed. "You've done so much for me already."

"Honey, it's just sitting in storage collecting dust," Edna waved a hand. "You'd be doing us a favor. If you don't like it, you can still shop for your own stuff."

"We should go shopping for what you still need!" Tracey started counting on her fingers. "Mattress, bedding, curtai ns..."

Katrina looked away before they could see the tears forming. This was what normal felt like. Women planning together, helping, caring. She'd forgotten what normal felt like.

"Do you need help with the deposit, honey?" Edna asked.

Katrina shook her head quickly. "No, I've got it covered. I have some savings." She glanced over at Ben, who hadn't said a word through all of this. His presence wasn't bothering her, but she wanted to know what he was thinking.

"When do you think you'll move in?" Tracey asked.

"Maybe next weekend? Once I sign the lease and everything clears."

Jayden appeared in the doorway, rubbing his eyes. "Mama, I'm tired."

Tracey stood. "Of course, baby. Let's get you a bath. Say good night to everyone."

Jayden gave a sleepy grin and then bowed, as if closing out on a stage play. "Goodnight, everybody."

The adults laughed.

Tracey shook her head. "My boy gets a bit dramatic around bedtime. Kat, we'll talk more tomorrow after you get a chance to look in storage. Goodnight, Ben."

Edna stood, groaning. "I need to put these old bones to bed. Kat, I'm so glad you're staying. Real glad." She touched Katrina's shoulder before exchanging a look with Ben. "Ben, feel free to stay longer. And thank you again for the new rocker."

The silence that settled after Edna went to the family quarters was deafening. Katrina found Ben staring at her. For a moment, the kitchen felt too small.

"The rental house is a good choice," Ben said finally. "I'm glad you're staying." He leaned back. "And I meant what I said yesterday. If you need help, I can help..."

Katrina's defenses went up. "I'm fine. I don't need—"

"With moving." He finished with a crooked smile. "I'm sure you need some muscle to help with moving furniture."

She let out a small laugh, feeling embarrassed. "Yes, I will need help, especially if Edna and Tracey have their way. Sounds like they have some cool stuff in storage."

"How was Savannah?"

Katrina tensed. "It was just business. Banking stuff for the rental."

"That makes sense." Ben nodded slowly. "Doing your business away from here."

She didn't answer. Instead, she stared at the table wondering how he knew.

"I'm not trying to get in your business," he said quietly. "I just... I recognize the signs."

Her voice came out smaller than she intended. "You don't know anything about me."

"No, I don't. But I can tell you're scared. And I think you're trying to cover your tracks."

The words escaped before she could stop them. "And what if I am? Why do you think you can help?"

He raised an eyebrow. "I'm a bit rusty. But I have ten years of law enforcement experience."

She sat back, suddenly too exhausted to keep pretending. "I went to Savannah to handle my finances. Get the cashier's check for the rental. But also..." She swallowed hard. "As you said, to cover my tracks. Make it harder for... for him to find me."

Ben leaned forward. "Who's *him*?"

"I can't say. But I do need help." Her voice broke on the words. "I'm worried about my aunt." She looked up at him, tears swimming in her eyes. "Her name is Lola. Lola Davis. She lives in Atlanta."

Ben sat up. "Is she in danger?"

"I don't know." Katrina's hands twisted in her lap. "The man I'm running from...he went to her house looking for me. She didn't answer the door, pretended she wasn't home. But he knows where she lives." Her voice dropped to almost a whisper. "I can't check on her properly. And I'm terrified he's going to keep hounding her to get to me."

Ben's expression shifted. "Does your aunt know you're here? In Beaufort?"

Katrina shook her head. "I told her I'm in a small town and I'm safe. That's all. I didn't give her details in case he tries to get information from her."

"That's smart." Ben rested his arms on the table. "Should we be worried about him showing up here?"

Katrina's eyes met his. "I don't know. But I'm not going to be staying at Sweetgrass anymore. And if I have to get another job..."

Ben's face turned hard, then softened. "You can't keep running. Look, I still have connections with Atlanta PD."

She nodded.

He glanced back at the Boyd's family quarters. "You don't seem willing to say his name. What can you tell me about him?"

Katrina took a shaky breath. Once she crossed this line, there was no going back. But she was so tired of being alone. So tired of being scared.

"He's..." She started, then had to stop. How could you explain Julian Cross to someone who'd never met him? "He's wealthy. Connected. Used to getting what he wants. He's very good with technology."

Ben raised an eyebrow.

"We dated for a few months. At first he seemed perfect." The words were coming easier now. "But then he knew things about me he shouldn't have known. I didn't even realize what he was doing."

Katrina couldn't tell Ben about the app. It all started with her downloading that stupid app on her phone. Then she'd encouraged her followers to download it too.

Ben's jaw tightened. "Did you go to the police?"

Katrina's laugh was harsh. "Are you kidding? You can't go to the police. Not on someone like *him*."

"So you ran."

She touched her short hair self-consciously. "I have tried to become invisible. But I can't have him going after my aunt. She's the only family I have left. I never thought he would go that far."

Ben reached out and touched her hand.

At first she wanted to snatch her hand back. But his touch, it felt warm and comforting.

"I can have someone do a welfare check without it being obvious. Drive by her house, make sure everything looks okay. If there's any sign of surveillance or trouble, they'll know what to look for."

Hope flickered in Katrina's chest. "You can do that?"

Ben nodded. "I'll make the call tomorrow. See what I can find out about your aunt."

"Thank you." The words felt inadequate for what he was offering.

"Get some rest. We'll talk more tomorrow."

Katrina stood too, suddenly aware of how exhausted she was. "Ben? Why are you helping me? You don't even know me."

He paused at the doorway, looking back at her. Something flickered across his face. "This is why I became a cop. To help people," he said quietly. "And because you shouldn't have to face this alone."

Then he was gone. Katrina wondered if she'd done the wrong thing confiding in Ben. She hadn't told him everything, but it was enough.

If he could help protect Aunt Lola, that was all that mattered.

And he was right about one thing.

I am so tired of being alone.

Chapter 16

Beaufort, South Carolina
Saturday, June 21 at 8:45 p.m.

As Ben drove away from Sweetgrass, his mind kept replaying the conversation with Kat. She'd actually asked him for help. He didn't know why that had touched him so deeply. It could have been because the past two weeks his instincts had been on point. His cop side had emerged, surprising him. He thought he'd buried that part of him the day Theo died.

Ben pulled into his driveway and cut the engine. For a long moment, he sat there, staring at his dark house. He'd told himself when he moved to Beaufort that he was done. Done with cases, done with investigating, done with the weight of other people's problems. He was a landscaper now. Someone who cut grass, and trimmed hedges, and minded his own business.

But Kat had looked at him with those frightened eyes and asked for his help.

And he'd said yes.

Because apparently, you could change your address, but you couldn't change who you were.

Ben climbed out of the truck and headed inside, flipping on lights as he went. Except for the hum of the refrigerator and the tick tock of the clock on the wall, the house was quiet. He stripped and headed for the shower, letting the cool water wash away the day's sweat and grime.

How easily could he slip back into his investigative side?

What did he actually know about Kat's situation? She and her Aunt Lola were from Atlanta. Kat was terrified enough to go into hiding. And now she was asking him for help.

Feeling refreshed, Ben headed to his bedroom and climbed into his king size bed. Even though it had been a long day, he wasn't ready for sleep. Kat had revealed enough to let him know he'd been right about her situation. But who was the culprit who'd made her life miserable enough for her to run, even going off the grid?

You can't go to the police? Not *on someone like him.*

Who was he? Kat described him as wealthy. That meant Kat thought he had the resources and the ability to track her down. Someone coming after her family to find her couldn't be a good person. But what happened between them?

Ben knew from experience people did crazy things to other people with no rhyme or reason. Sometimes it was just because they could.

His eyes drifted to his phone. It was after nine now, too late to be calling anyone. But his sleeping habits had never really changed. He slept lightly or not at all.

The person he had in mind to call would answer the phone. If Kat trusted him enough to ask for help, he needed to get on this now. He needed eyes in Atlanta. And there was only one person he could think of who might help.

Ben picked up his phone, thumb hovering over Jenna's contact. He'd saved her number after the call about Theo's case. He'd been tempted to reach out to see if there had been any updates, but he knew it was best he stay out of it.

He sighed, then pressed the call button before he could change his mind.

It rang once. Twice. On the third ring, she answered with a sleepy, "Hello."

He cleared his throat. "Jenna, it's me. Ben."

Her voice alert. "Ben? Everything okay?"

"Yeah. I'm sorry to call so late."

A soft laugh came through the line. "I was wondering what took you so long to call back."

Ben blinked. "What?"

"Come on, Ben. I've known you for what, ten years? I also know how close you were to Theo. I'm actually impressed you waited this long to call for details."

Ben felt a smile tug at his lips. "You always did know me too well, but that's not why I'm calling."

"Oh." Her tone sounded surprised. "You're not interested?"

"I didn't say that."

Jenna chuckled. "I don't remember you being this coy, Ben Wyatt. You didn't have a problem asking or getting what you wanted."

That was before.

"I've changed a lot, Jenna."

"I see." Her voice softened. "We're making real progress. I wanted you to know that."

Ben closed his eyes, letting himself feel it… Hope. "Thanks, Jenna. For staying on it."

"Of course. Now you said you called for another reason?"

He ran a hand over his jaw. "There's a woman staying at the bed-and-breakfast where I do yard work. Her name's Kat. Kat Miles, so she says."

"Okay. You sound like you don't believe that's her name."

"I don't. I got the sense she was running for someone. She confirmed tonight and asked me for help. She knows I'm an ex-cop."

Jenna asked. "What do you need from me?"

Ben appreciated that she didn't hesitate. "She mentioned her aunt. A woman named Lola Davis."

There was a sharp intake of breath on the other end of the line.

"Jenna?"

"Did you say Lola Davis?"

Ben swung his legs off the bed, adrenaline flowing. "Yeah. You know her?"

“Know her?” Jenna’s voice turned incredulous. “If it’s the Lola Davis I know, I attended the Lola Davis Dance Academy. She’s a legendary dancer and choreographer.”

It was Ben’s turn to be surprised. “You danced?”

Jenna laughed. “What a question. Yes, from age seven to twelve. Best and worst years of my childhood.” Her tone changed, more serious. “You said this woman called Lola her aunt.”

“That’s right.” Ben buzzed with the small world connection. “Do you remember a Kat in Lola’s life?”

“I don’t remember the niece’s name, but I remember a young girl who came to the dance studio to be around Lola a lot. I also remember that Lola took her niece in after her sister died.”

Ben’s body stilled. “What happened?”

“Oh my. It was a really tragic car accident. Drunk driver. Killed both parents. Lola became the guardian. If this Kat is her niece, and she’s in trouble, Lola would move heaven and earth to protect her.”

Ben thought about Kat’s fearful plea for help. “Kat is concerned the guy who’s been... I guess stalking her is now harassing her aunt to find her.”

Jenna sucked in a breath. “Tell me no more. I will check on Lola as soon as possible. Make it casual, you know, like a former student dropping by to say hello. Lola always loved when her dancers came back to visit.”

Some of the tension in his shoulders eased.

"Ben, if this girl is running from something serious enough to leave her whole life behind and her aunt is Lola Davis," Jenna's voice softened, "who did she get involved with?"

"I'm hoping you can find that out. Kat stayed pretty vague. I got the impression it was a wealthy person, a mover and shaker in Atlanta. Maybe not someone you run to the police about."

"Got it. I'll call you after I visit Lola. It will probably be Tuesday or Wednesday, but I'll feel out the situation, see if she mentions her niece."

"Thank you, Jenna. I appreciate it."

"Of course." She paused. "And, Ben? It's really good to hear your voice."

Ben looked down at his hands, at the calluses from working with wood and landscaping tools. "Yeah. It's good to talk to you too."

"Be careful down there," Jenna said.

"I'll keep an eye out. I haven't lost my skills."

"I'm sure you haven't." There was a smile in her voice. "Goodnight, Ben."

"Goodnight, Jenna."

Ben ended the call. Sitting on the side of his bed with the phone still in his hand, he thought about the connections threading through his life like invisible lines. Theo's case connecting him back to Jenna. Jenna connecting to Lola Davis. Lola connecting to Kat. If he had a whiteboard, he'd map out all the connections and draw arrows. Theo used to tease him about his determination to connect everything.

Ben stood and walked to the window, looking out at the dark street. He'd come to Beaufort to get away from all of this. To leave behind the detective work, the cases, and the weight of trying to save people.

And not being able to save them.

Losing his partner. His best friend.

But you couldn't outrun who you were. And apparently, who he was, who he'd always been, was someone who couldn't walk away when someone asked for help.

Ben was determined not to let Kat down.

Chapter 17

Beaufort, South Carolina
Saturday, June 21 at 9:30 p.m.

Katrina sat on the edge of her bed with her arms crossed in front of her, still processing what had happened over an hour ago. As the adrenaline built up from the day trip to Savannah crashed, she drew in a shaky breath and tried to stop her body from trembling. She was so tired of being afraid. Katrina felt compelled to ask Ben for help, for some relief.

Did I make a mistake?

No. She'd considered that Julian might try to find her, but she couldn't have him harassing Aunt Lola. He hadn't taken too kindly to her threat to expose him. Instead, he ramped up his intimidation tactics, tracking her every move. It's why she had to leave her old life.

But Julian had no idea who he was messing with either. Lola Davis was kind of like royalty in the African American community in Atlanta. Everyone knew the former dancer. It was competitive to get accepted to the Lola Davis Dance

Company. Even being Lola's niece, Katrina still had to audition and dance just as hard as the other dancers. Many women and men who'd gone through that school still lived and worked in Atlanta.

Katrina knew her feisty Gen X aunt would fight back to protect her niece. She heard it in her aunt's voice. But Aunt Lola didn't know or understand what Julian could do. She wasn't aware of his sneaky tactics, using his vast resources to track, hack, and destroy. Julian Cross wasn't the polished businessman he claimed to be.

Katrina could no longer think only of herself. That is why when Ben looked at her with those steady, patient eyes, she instinctively knew she could trust him. He'd get someone in Atlanta to look out for Aunt Lola.

She fell back on the bed, letting the fluffy comforter envelop her as she stared up at the ceiling. If only she'd refused Julian's offer. His sponsorship opportunity was something new and exciting beyond what she usually did with Black hair care and makeup. She should've just stuck to what had always been her niche under @KatsGlowUp.

Tears stung her eyes, spilling down her cheeks.

She'd started that Instagram account when she was nineteen and, later, her YouTube channel. The following year, she jumped on the TikTok craze during the pandemic. Six years of hard work. Her way of fighting back the depression that swallowed her after losing her parents. In a way, it's what kept her focused and going. That and Aunt Lola's encouragement.

Katrina sat up suddenly and grabbed her phone from the nightstand. A new idea sparked. She wasn't helpless. Hadn't she slipped away from him? And she'd also built an entire career on tracking engagement metrics, studying algorithms, and understanding online behavior patterns.

It was time for her to track the man who'd caused her so much misery.

Two can play this game.

Of course, she didn't have the programmers and sophisticated software, but she knew Julian's weaknesses. What she was thinking of doing would be doable on her burner phone. She could borrow Tracey's laptop, but she would have to be careful to erase her history. No, once she got her own place, she would plan to get a laptop, maybe a Chromebook.

Katrina opened the Gmail app on her phone browser. She needed to create a new account. Should she use something close to her name or something entirely different? After a few moments of thinking, a memory floated through her mind.

She'd been about six or seven years old and had just started dancing in Aunt Lola's dance academy. After class, she would float around the house, showing off her new dance steps. Her mother would smile and call her "Little bird."

With her mother's voice in her ear, the username came to her. She typed: LittleBird2000@gmail.com

Her fingers hesitated over the confirmation button. Creating a fake account felt like crossing a line. But it was nothing compared to the way Julian spied on people with his app. She pressed confirm.

Now that she had a new email, next was Instagram. Out of all the social networks, Julian hung out on Instagram the most. She opened the app and clicked "Create New Account." She thought through another username. In her world, branding had been so important. This didn't matter. She was creating an account designed to be invisible.

Katrina decided to stick with the same @littlebird2000.

No profile picture. The default gray silhouette stared back at her. No bio. No posts. No followers. No following.

The irony wasn't lost on her with how many times she looked at her almost 90,000 followers on Instagram and saw so many of these faceless profiles following her.

For a moment, she was tempted to log into her real accounts. @KatsGlowUp was still out there, invisible to the world. The accounts existed in some digital limbo, waiting for her return. Her DMs were probably full. Comments piling up on her last posts from three weeks ago, and her followers wondering where she'd gone.

She could check. Just once. See what people were saying. See if any brands had reached out.

No. Logging into @KatsGlowUp would leave a digital footprint. A timestamp. A location ping.

One day, maybe. When Julian was out of her life. When she was safe again. Maybe then she could reactivate everything and explain to her followers what had happened.

But not today.

Today, she was @littlebird2000. And she had work to do.

She navigated to the search bar, her heart pounding, and typed Julian Cross.

His account appeared immediately at the top of the results. That polished profile photo, the one from his *Forbes* feature. Perfectly lit, professionally taken. The image of success.

@LifeTrackCEO: Entrepreneur. Innovator. TED Speaker. @LifeTrackApp CEO Building the future, one innovation at a time. 145K followers.

Seeing his face on her screen made her stomach churn. That smile. A year ago, he'd charmed her that night at the St. Regis Atlanta. Now, when she looked into those intense green eyes, all she saw was a narcissist. Maybe even a sociopath.

She clicked through to his profile, scouring the most recent posts. It appeared he'd posted about seven days ago with a photo of him inside his ultra-modern office with its expensive furniture.

Staying focused on innovation even when the world feels chaotic. The best ideas come when you block out the noise. #EntrepreneurLife #StayFocused #LifeTrackApp

Katrina rolled her eyes. "He thinks he's some motivational guru now."

She continued to scroll down, taking in Julian's carefully curated feed.

@LifeTrackCEO: A selfie of Julian flexing his arm, showing off muscles under a white t-shirt. *Discipline is choosing between what you want now and what you want most. #FitnessJourney #MindsetMatters #LifeTrackApp*

@LifeTrackCEO: Julian holding a mug of coffee, standing in front of his expensive espresso machine. *Starting the day right. Small rituals, big impact. #MorningRoutine #Productivity #LifeTrackApp*

@LifeTrackCEO: Julian shaking hands with other men in expensive suits, all of them smiling. *Grateful to connect with fellow innovators at last night's Tech Leaders Summit. Are you using the @LifeTrackApp yet? #Networking #TechCommunity*

Nothing but selfies.

"He always thought he was so important. That he was doing great things."

Katrina sighed, wondering for the hundredth time how she got caught up with *this man*.

And that app. She'd promoted LifeTrack to her followers.

She muttered, "More like #LifeTRAP!"

That's what she'd figured out too late. Deleting LifeTrack didn't actually remove location tracking. The app left some kind of digital fingerprint that Julian's programmers could still access.

He was able to track her even after she'd deleted the Life-Track App from her phone.

It's why she had to throw everything away. Her apartment. Her Audi. Her MacBook. Her smartphone. Katrina had contemplated deleting her entire online presence.

How long could she really remain hidden from him?

What would he do if he found me?

Chapter 18

Second Baptist Church
Sunday, June 22 at 11:30 a.m.

Something in Katrina shifted last night. She'd been hiding from everything. Even God. But last night, she stopped running and started fighting back. She had a plan now. A way to watch Julian, to track his movements, to know where he was before he found her.

Katrina was confident that God was guiding her. That she no longer needed to drown in hopelessness.

"Won't he do it! Won't God do it!"

Katrina smiled as she watched Edna stand, shout, and raise her hands. She'd never seen the motherly bed-and-breakfast owner dressed outside of her usual uniform. Today, Edna wore a purple suit and donned a wide-brimmed purple hat to match. For the first time since arriving in Beaufort, Katrina joined the Boyds at their church. She sat on one side of Edna while Tracey and Jayden sat on the other side. Katrina found

Edna liked to sit close to the front. Tracey teased, saying the second row on the left was known as Edna's pew.

Thankfully, Katrina had kept some dresses and found a yellow dress that hung right above her knees. It was a dress she'd picked out on a shopping excursion with her Aunt Lola. She remembered that day vividly. Katrina had grown used to purchasing most items online, but Aunt Lola insisted they go to Macy's at Lenox Square Mall. They shopped like they'd done when she was younger, before becoming an influencer.

While the dress she wore today was modern, more for a twenty-something year old, the dress reminded her of one she'd worn when she was six-years old. She had a photo that she'd kept of her standing next to her mother. Something about this yellow dress made her feel closer to her mother. Katrina fingered the locket around her neck. Her father had given it to her on her thirteenth birthday. Though her parents's graves were back in Atlanta, she felt close to them today, anchored by her memories.

The Second Baptist Church was very different from the megachurch she'd attended. The white clapboard building was half full, but the energy felt like there was a stadium full of people.

The preacher, an older man with thick black glasses and a graying bald head, wiped sweat from his head with a large white handkerchief as he finished his sermon. In perfect sync, the choir stood when the preacher took his seat.

Great is Thy faithfulness, Lord unto me.

The tears came quietly, but Katrina didn't fight them. Edna grabbed her hand and placed a tissue in her other palm. Katrina looked over at the woman, grateful for her strength. Once again, she felt like God had led her to this place, to Sweetgrass, to be under Edna's guidance. The Lowcountry had become a sanctuary.

After the service, Katrina noticed Ben. She hadn't realized he'd been sitting a few rows behind them. He looked very different today in a gray pinstripe suit with a red tie. He appeared even more handsome. Katrina wondered if this was how he dressed when he used to be a detective. Their eyes met, and he gave her a small wave.

Katrina was glad to see him and hoped he had some news about her aunt. Unfortunately, she lost sight of Ben as congregation members came up to Edna and Tracey, curious about Katrina and introducing themselves.

"Are you visiting?"

"How long are you staying?"

"Where are you from?"

After meeting a blur of faces, including Pastor Williams, they finally landed outside the church, huddled together on the sidewalk.

"Good afternoon, ladies." Ben walked up to the group. He gave Jayden a fist bump first.

"Looking sharp today, young man. I like the bowtie."

Jayden grinned. "Thanks, Mr. Ben."

She patted him on his shoulders. “Good to see you this morning, Ben.”

Tracey clasped her hands together. “I just saw the double rocker this morning. You did such a beautiful job on it.”

“Didn’t he! This young man is so talented.” Edna beamed at Ben. “You can do another business with your woodworking skills.”

“No, no. I will stick to the landscaping. The woodworking is just a hobby.” He eyed Katrina. “Can I borrow you for a second?”

Katrina felt her eyes widen in surprise. “Um, sure.”

Edna and Tracey gave her encouraging nods and knowing smiles. She wasn’t sure what to think of their expressions, but Katrina stepped aside with Ben, away from the groups of people standing around talking.

“I reached out to a former colleague last night,” Ben said, his voice low enough that only she could hear. “Detective Jenna Cole in Atlanta. She will check on your aunt.”

Relief washed through Katrina so suddenly her knees felt weak. “Thank you. You moved really fast.”

“I understood the urgency.”

Their eyes held for a moment, something passing between them that made Katrina feel a warmth that didn’t have anything to do with being outside in the afternoon sun.

Then a bright voice cut through the moment. “Ben Wyatt, you’re a hard man to pin down.”

Michelle Carver appeared at Ben's elbow, her hand slid into his arm. She wore a coral dress that showed off a fit body.

Ben shifted and patted Michelle's hand before gently dislodging her arm from his. "Michelle. Good to see you."

Michelle seemed to notice Katrina for the first time. "Oh! Kat! I'm so glad I ran into you. I showed the house yesterday to a couple from Charleston. They seemed interested."

The bottom dropped out of Katrina's stomach. Of course someone else would want it.

Michelle reached over and touched her arm. "Honestly, though? I think it really fits *you*. The couple wanted to see three more places before deciding."

Katrina spoke quickly. "I was going to call you Monday. I want to put down the deposit and four months of rent."

Michelle's eyes widened. "Oh, that's wonderful! We could get the paperwork started this afternoon if you'd like. No need to wait until tomorrow."

"Yes, this afternoon would be great."

"Perfect." Michelle pulled out her phone. "I can meet you at my office at three o'clock? I'll have everything ready to go—lease agreement, move-in checklist, the works." Then she paused, studying Katrina's face. "You know, Kat, I keep feeling like I've seen you somewhere before we met at the showing."

Ben shifted beside them. Katrina could feel his gaze on her.

"I just have one of those faces, I guess," Katrina said with a forced laugh.

"That could be true." She shook her head. "Never mind. Sorry for sounding crazy." Michelle laughed. "Well, anyway, three o'clock?"

"Three o'clock sounds good," Katrina confirmed. She was relieved Michelle dropped the subject so fast. For a moment, Katrina wondered if the woman really recognized her. That would ruin everything.

"Wonderful," Michelle said, her hand returning to Ben's arm as she prepared to leave. "I'll see you then, Kat. And, Ben, don't be such a stranger." Her touch lingered a moment on Ben's arm before she headed toward the parking lot.

Ben turned his body to face Katrina, blocking her from seeing Michelle's exit.

Katrina gulped. She thought Ben might question her more about Michelle thinking she'd seen her before. With Ben standing so close, she caught a whiff of his cologne, distracting her.

Man, he smells good. Looks good too!

He grinned. "That's great about the house. I'm glad you're staying around."

"Yes. I really fell in love with it on Friday."

"Let me know when move-in day will be. I'll be there."

"Thank you! And thank you again for reaching out to your friend in Atlanta. I appreciate her checking on Aunt Lola."

Ben held her gaze for a moment. "Not a problem. I will be in touch as soon as I hear something." He gave her a salute. "Enjoy your afternoon."

Her eyes followed Ben as he headed toward the familiar truck. So intent on watching him, Katrina was startled to see Tracey, Jayden, and Edna appear on either side of her.

"Well, now," Edna said, "Sounds like we need to help you get setup in your new place."

Tracey linked her arm through Katrina's. "You'd be surprised what Aunt Edna's got stored away. We could furnish half the town with what's up in that attic."

Edna nodded. "I hope you will find something you can use. With Ben's help, we can move things whenever you're ready."

Katrina looked between them, overwhelmed by their generosity. "I really can't thank you both enough for all that you've done for me."

Edna started walking toward the parking lot. "I just hope that you will find some peace."

Peace. That was definitely something Katrina longed for.

Following the Boyd family back to Tracey's car, Julian felt very far away at this moment. But Katrina knew better.

She'd check Julian's accounts again tonight. Map his movements. She needed to stay one step ahead.

Chapter 19

Beaufort, South Carolina
Sunday, June 22 at 3:30 p.m.

Ben drove back to his house from church, and his mind settled on Michelle Carver. But not for reasons the overly aggressive woman expected. He found it curious that Michelle thought she'd seen Kat before. Ben considered bringing it up once Michelle left, but he could tell Kat had been rattled. He figured he would find another opportunity to talk to her. What was most important was to make sure Kat stayed in town. He couldn't help protect her if she fled.

And why am I so bent on protecting her?

He knew why. From the moment she showed up at the Sweetgrass, he'd been drawn to her like a moth to light. It wasn't just a physical attraction.

He considered reaching out to Michelle to find out more, but that was a trap waiting to be sprung. That woman was too determined to get him in her clutches. Like Edna, Michelle had brought him considerable clientele through her realtor company, so Ben didn't want to hurt the woman's feelings. But she would never succeed.

Ben arrived home and changed into a comfortable t-shirt and jeans. He slipped his phone inside his pocket and headed to work on another project. Out in the garage, he looked at the wooden shapes he had on the table. Jayden joked about making a car, but Ben had thought through the plans. Laid out on the table was the beginning shape of a sports car. Ben would bring over the pieces so that he and Jayden could assemble the car at the Sweetgrass.

His phone buzzed inside his pocket. He pulled out the phone and froze. Jenna's name flashed on the screen.

"Hey," he answered. "That was fast."

"Yeah, I was able to connect with Ms. Davis this morning. We talked for a while. I've got Atlanta PD doing regular drive-bys." Jenna's voice was tight. "Ben, we need to talk."

His body stilled at the tone of Jenna's voice. "What did Ms. Davis say?"

Jenna blew out a breath. "She spilled everything. And she's terrified for her niece."

"Did she say why?"

"First, her niece's name is Katrina Bowen."

Kat. Katrina.

Ben commented, "She stuck close to her real name."

"Yeah. Well, it might've been easier. The easiest thing that woman has done. Ms. Davis told me everything happened so fast. Katrina is twenty-seven years old and until a month ago, she'd been a big-time beauty influencer on social media. Apparently, she met up with Julian Cross about a year ago. Her aunt didn't fully understand her niece's life as an influencer, but she understood Katrina helped promote Julian's app. She thought they dated for a while."

Ben's pulse quickened. The name Julian Cross sounded familiar to him, but he wanted to know more about what Jenna had found out. "Go on."

"Ms. Davis said that Katrina suddenly made her social media disappear, like maybe she deleted or hid it all. The woman had hundreds of thousands of followers. In fact, folks are talking about her online wondering why she suddenly disappeared. Anyway, Ms. Davis said that Katrina got rid of her car, broke the lease on her apartment and even cut her hair."

Ben swallowed. "Good Lord! What did he do to her?"

"Her aunt wasn't sure because Katrina didn't tell her. But I gathered he must have been stalking her. Ms. Davis told me how Julian showed up at her house at least two times. She said the last time he showed up, he scared her. I'm about to send you a photo of her Ring camera. This guy is a real creep."

His phone pinged, and Ben pulled up his text.

A dark blond haired man with intense green eyes stared back at him. The smile on the man's face angered Ben. He'd seen that type of smile before. On criminals who thought they were above the law. Who had no remorse after committing crimes.

Jenna's voice penetrated his growing anger. "I looked up Julian Cross and researched his LifeTrack app. Ben, I found a connection with Theo's case."

Ben thought he heard Jenna wrong. "What did you say?"

"The LifeTrack app launched publicly about a year ago, but it was in development before that. It's marketed as a lifestyle app. You can keep up with your schedule, journal, and even create videos. Folks who use it often use it to record personal stuff. It also can share your locations and check in with other people."

Ben's mind raced, still trying to figure out where Jenna saw the connection to Theo's case. "Sounds like most social media, but with a few bells and whistles. Not sure what makes it so special." He added a bit impatiently. "And what's the connection to the case Theo and I were investigating?"

Jenna was quiet for a moment. "The case you guys were working on was a human trafficking ring, right?"

Ben swallowed. "Yes. We were closing in on someone we thought was holding women."

"Right. There was a shell company that kept coming up. Horizon Capital Partner. That same company is listed as one of LifeTrack's investors."

Ben felt like someone had punched him in the stomach. The investor they'd been circling but couldn't touch. He shook his head. "I don't understand. Are you saying something is funny about this app?"

Jenna sighed. "I don't know, but I think we need you to find out why Katrina took off the way she did."

He looked up toward the garage ceiling as he caught where Jenna was going with this conversation. "You think she knows something?"

"Hear me out. This is just a theory. And it may go nowhere. But what if Katrina figured out or saw something that scared her? If Julian Cross is connected to the same people who killed Theo..."

"She's in danger." Ben rubbed his hand across his head. This was worse than he thought.

"Do you think she will talk to you? Tell you what she knows."

"I can try, but I'm not a cop anymore, Jenna."

"Sometimes that's better. Sounds like you've already developed a rapport with her."

Had he? She reached out to him for help.

Ben wasn't sure what that meant. Kat could have just been desperate to protect her aunt. His shoulders sagged. "I will let you know if she tells me anything."

"Good. I'll call you when I know more on my end."

"Thanks, Jenna."

He hung up and stood for a long time, staring at nothing in particular.

Katrina Bowen.

How much did she know about Julian Cross? How did this connect back to the case that took his partner's life?

Part Three

The Reckoning

Chapter 20

Beaufort, South Carolina
Tuesday, June 23 at 3:00 p.m.

Katrina stood in the middle of her new living room, admiring the transformation she'd managed in just two days. Having the living room furnished already had been a real blessing. Sunlight streamed through the light gray curtains she'd found at the local bargain store. Almost reminiscent of her former apartment, she'd been able to find colorful throw pillows she scattered across the gray sofa adding pops of color.

Excitement she hadn't experienced in months sprung in her body as her eyes fell on the inexpensive canvas paintings of mocha colored women. She found some heavy duty sticky tape for walls and installed the canvases around the living room. The little house felt more and more like her.

Her house. For the next four months at least, paid in full.

She'd signed the lease Sunday afternoon and handed Michelle the cashier's check that she'd withdrawn while in

Savannah. Now she just needed Ben to arrive so they could tackle the bed frame and headboard she'd found in Edna's storage. Edna and Tracey weren't kidding when they told her about all the items they had in storage.

Katrina instantly fell in love with the white headboard, which reminded her of the one in the Blue room at the Sweetgrass.

A knock at the front door made her turn. Through the window by the door, she caught sight of Ben standing on the porch. He wore his usual work clothes, faded jeans and an olive green t-shirt that had seen better days. He'd grown on her in the past few weeks. Normally, she paid little attention to men with beards, but Ben had captured her attention. His beard sculpted his face, and his brown eyes always displayed warmth, even when they seemed to question her.

She opened the door, gesturing for him to come inside. Katrina closed the door and turned toward him. "Hey, Ben. I really appreciate you helping me out."

He flashed her a wide grin. "Not a problem. We can't have you sleeping on the floor."

Before she could stop herself, she'd started giggling. "I slept on the couch last night, it wasn't too bad."

He glanced over at the couch and then his eyes roamed the room. "Wow. You spruced up this place fast. Everything looks great!"

Katrina felt warmth spread through her chest. "Thank you." She wasn't sure why she felt so flattered. Ben made her feel like she could trust a man again. And she needed that right now.

They worked together, taking turns, Ben holding pieces in place while Katrina tightened bolts. Their hands brushed more than once. Each time, she felt that flutter in her stomach that she'd been trying to ignore for weeks.

"There," Ben said finally, stepping back to survey their work. He bounced on the edge of the mattress they'd just placed on the frame. "Sturdy. You won't be falling through in the middle of the night."

Katrina looked around the bedroom, taking in the afternoon light filtering through the blinds. She had white curtains that she would add before she went to bed. And the empty walls were ready for some touches too. She'd bought canvases with flowers and butterflies.

"You need help with anything else?" Ben asked.

"Not right now. Thank you," she said quietly. "For all this. For helping me."

"Not a problem."

"Mind if I check your windows real quick? Old habit from the force."

Katrina followed him as he did a quick walk through the small house. When he tried the back door, testing the handle, he frowned slightly.

"This lock's pretty basic. Just a handle lock, no deadbolt." He glanced at her. "Ask Michelle about upgrading it. Not trying to scare you, but it wouldn't take much to get through this."

Katrina looked at the simple back door lock and made a mental note. "I will. Just trying to settle in first. Get the basics done."

Ben nodded. "Fair enough. Just... be careful, okay?"

She looked at him. He gazed back at her. Something passed between them.

Ben is a real gentleman. He makes things so easy.

Her heart began to beat faster.

She stepped back. "I should feed you. It's the least I can do after putting you to work all afternoon."

Ben stood and shook his head. "You don't have to—"

"We both have to eat dinner. How do you feel about Chinese food? Do you have a favorite place around here?"

"I do. But let this be my treat. I can DoorDash it. Okay?"

She started to protest, but realized it was probably a better idea for Ben to order. She hadn't even thought about food delivery, which she missed and used to do all the time back in Atlanta.

Forty minutes later, they sat at the cozy kitchen table that also was gifted from the Sweetgrass storage. Like the headboard, she fell in love with the quaintness of the small four seat table. The white wood furnishing reminded her of Aunt Lola's cozy kitchen nook, with its white banquette nestled in front of the window, overlooking the backyard. Katrina had spent many evenings in her aunt's kitchen working on homework, and later starting her @KatsGlowUp brand.

Even though she'd gotten dishes from Edna, she picked up paper plates and plastic utensils. Another old habit. Ben had already dived into his orange chicken. It wasn't the first time she had eaten in front of him, but they were alone. No Edna, Tracey, or Jayden.

She'd kept it simple with shrimp fried rice and an egg roll. Her excitement for the new place began to be replaced with the growing anxiety that plagued her. Had she done the right thing settling here? Atlanta was only five hours away.

Ben's velvety deep voice broke into her thoughts. "Is the food okay? You seem really quiet."

Should she tell him everything? Ben had been a godsend to her, getting the Atlanta PD to check on Aunt Lola. But the words stuck in her throat. All she could do was smile and nod.

Ben pushed his plate away. "I wanted to talk to you about something."

Katrina's pulse quickened. "Okay."

"You already know I was a detective in Atlanta. My partner was Theo Mason. Good man. Best partner I ever had." Ben stared down at the table. "He was killed three years ago during what was supposed to be surveillance on a case."

"Ben, I'm so sorry." She thought back to a conversation she'd overheard a few weeks ago. "Was that anniversary fairly recent?"

He nodded. "June 6. The same day you showed up in Beaufort."

"Oh." That was all she could say; she wasn't sure where Ben was going with his reveal.

He continued. "I left the force after. Couldn't stay. Couldn't face his family, couldn't..." He trailed off. "Anyway, when I talked Detective Jenna Cole about your aunt, something else came up."

Katrina's stomach dropped. She dropped her fork, not realizing it was still in her hand. She'd been so focused on Ben.

He looked at her. "I know that you're Katrina Bowen."

Katrina leaned back against the chair and closed her eyes. "So this detective spoke to my aunt, didn't she?"

"I told you we would check on her. That would mean a wellness check in person."

She couldn't breathe properly. Couldn't think. She stuttered, "Wh-what did my aunt say?"

"She was very proud of her niece, the influencer who'd built up quite a brand and then... just disappeared. Left everything behind without explanation."

Tears sprang to her eyes. She didn't want to do this. Not in front of him.

"Your aunt's worried about you." His voice was gentle. "She told Jenna about some guy you were with. Julian Cross. He owns the LifeTrack app."

Her vision blurred at the edges. She was going to be sick. Katrina placed her hands around her head.

"Kat, look at me."

She shut her eyes tight like some petulant child. Then she snapped them open to face the man across from her. Katrina expected to see anger for her lies, but all she saw was the same kindness in Ben's eyes he'd shown her since she arrived.

"I knew you were in trouble when you arrived," Ben said. He leaned forward slightly, his eyes searching her face. "Tell me what happened. What did Julian do?"

The question hung in the air between them.

Katrina's throat closed. Then something occurred to her, making her angry. "How long have you known?"

Ben sat back. "Since I talked to Jenna two days ago. After church on Sunday."

Two days. He'd known for two days and had said nothing. Hadn't confronted her at work, hadn't told Edna, hadn't—

"Why didn't you say something before now?"

"Because I wanted you to feel safe." Ben eyed her. "I wanted you to have this. Your own place. I couldn't help you if you ran off."

Katrina felt something crack open inside her chest and stood abruptly, needing distance. She walked into the living room and wrapped her arms around herself, against a chill that didn't exist. At least not physically.

Behind her, she heard Ben stand too, but he didn't come closer.

“Kat,” he said. “If you’re in danger. I want to help. This man. Julian Cross. I can tell he’s not a good guy. I got a look at his face on your aunt’s Ring camera.”

Katrina spun around and realized Ben was coming toward her, his phone in his hand.

“Is this him?” Ben turned the screen around to face her.

Katrina’s breath came fast as her eyes locked on Julian. Behind him, Katrina recognized her aunt’s neighbor’s house across the street. He’d been at her aunt’s house looking for her. Anger kindled as she focused on the man’s face. That arrogant smile!

I want this man out of my life.

She glared at Ben, unable to contain her rage.

“I’ll tell you everything about Julian Cross.”

Chapter 21

Beaufort, South Carolina
Tuesday, June 23 at 5:45 p.m.

Ben watched Kat stare at his phone screen. A startling transformation happened across her beautiful face. Eyes filled with fear focused on the image on his phone. Then, as if a light had switched on, her brown eyes flashed with fierce anger. Ben knew that feeling, when helplessness ran up against a raging desire to make something happen. Anything to stop the madness.

Kat looked away from the screen, her arms wrapping tighter around herself. When she finally met his eyes, something had shifted in her face. A decision made.

"I'll tell you everything about Julian Cross."

"Let's sit down." Ben pocketed his phone and moved to the couch. Kat stayed standing for a moment, then she sat on the opposite end, leaving space between them. She grabbed one of the throw pillows and held it against her body like a shield.

“I’m just going to listen,” Ben said. “No judgment. No interruptions unless I need clarification. Okay?”

She nodded. “Seems like you already know I’m @Kats-GlowUp online, aka Katrina Bowen,” she began. “I have about two hundred thousand followers across platforms. Brand partnerships. Sponsorships. It was my full-time job for almost six years.”

Ben kept his expression neutral, but Kat impressed him even more. Two hundred thousand followers. That was a legitimate business.

“I met Julian at an influencer gala last June. A year ago.” Kat stated. “It was at the St. Regis in Atlanta. He was the keynote speaker. Featured in *Forbes*, TED Talk, you name it. He launched the LifeTrack app officially at that gala. A beta version had been out for a few years.”

“My thing was natural hair care products, some makeup and beauty products. I started another YouTube channel where I focused more on interior design, decor…” She looked around her living room and smiled. “You know, stuff like this. Decorating, making your place your home.”

He smiled. “You have a real talent there. I love what you’ve done to this place in such a short amount of time.”

She smiled back at him, but quickly became serious again. Almost sad.

Ben waited patiently, not wanting to push her. This woman had stopped her whole life, tried to rebuild it within a few weeks, to run away from this man.

"He approached me. Julian. I was surprised, but he'd convinced me I would be a good fit. I had the lifestyle crowd, and he'd get authentic promotion from a trusted influencer." She paused. "The commission alone was more than I'd made in six months from any other deals."

Ben asked, "How did this app work?"

She hesitated. "At first, I really loved the app. It helped me schedule posts, track my fitness, and manage my calendar. I promoted it genuinely. My followers trusted my recommendations." Her voice went flat. "What I didn't realize was how much access I was giving him."

Alarm bells went off in Ben's head. "What do you mean?"

"This past October. We'd been working together for a couple of months. He invited me to his lake house on Lake Lanier." Kat's fingers twisted together. "That's when things shifted. He started being pushy about me using the app. I guess I hadn't been doing as much promotion."

"So he was showing some aggression."

"I guess. I didn't think too much of it. But at the beginning of the year, I started noticing things were off. At first, I thought I was being paranoid and forgetting stuff. I was busy trying to keep up with my content schedule. But I realized Julian would show up in places I hadn't told him about. Know things about my day I hadn't shared. One time, he tracked me down at a coffee shop in Midtown. Said he'd been trying to call, couldn't reach me, got worried. Made it sound like an emergency."

"So, there was no emergency?" Ben said.

"No. He just wanted to see me. And when I asked how he found me, he said LifeTrack showed him where I was. But the weird thing was, I wasn't sharing my location. At least I thought I wasn't." Kat looked up at Ben. "He turned it around on me. Made me feel guilty for not being available immediately. Said if I trusted him, I wouldn't have a problem with transparency."

Classic manipulation. And what was up with that app?

"Did you try to delete the app?"

Kat sat up, clutching the throw pillow harder. "I deleted LifeTrack completely from my phone in late April."

"Let me guess. It didn't matter."

She whispered, her eyes focused on him. "No. Ben, even deleted, it must have been running in the background. Still tracking." Kat's voice cracked. "I confronted Julian about it, and he said it was for my protection. What if someone stole my phone? What if something happened to me? It would enable me to be found. That's when it hit me. All these folks I'd touted this app too. They weren't aware of what it could do. How it invaded your privacy."

Ben's hands curled into fists against his thighs. Julian Cross had built the technology that could infiltrate people's privacy. And one of his investors, Horizon Capital Partner, had been involved in a human trafficking ring.

This was so much bigger than Ben had expected.

"I told him I wanted to take a break from promoting LifeTrack. That I needed distance from the app and from him." She turned to face Ben, her eyes bright with unshed tears. "He got angry. Really angry. He didn't touch me physically then, but he started stalking me in a weird way."

Ben tilted his head. "What do you mean weird?"

Her voice broke. "In my DMs, I would see screenshots of my messages. Private conversations with my aunt and friends. There would be texts of photos I had posted nowhere. I knew it was him."

Ben stared. "How did you know it was him?"

"At first, I thought maybe my phone got hacked. But..." She stopped, swallowing hard. "Then I remembered his face when I told him I didn't want to promote the LifeTrack app."

Ben leaned toward her. "How did he react?"

She shrugged. "He laughed at first. Said I was overreacting, being dramatic. Then, when he realized I was serious, he got cold. Told me I couldn't just walk away. That we had a contract. I'd signed agreements to be a brand ambassador for LifeTrack. If I backed out, he'd sue me for breach of contract and damages."

Ben sighed as dread built inside his chest. "Did you have a lawyer look at the contract?"

"No, but I should have." She leaned back on the couch, looking exhausted. "My brand has been my identity and my livelihood for six years. And I marketed that horrible app to so many people. I felt ashamed."

That's when you decided to run?"

"Yes! I deactivated my social media, packed up my apartment, and sold a lot of stuff, even my car. For him to track me down at my aunt's house, that was classic stalking. Then he had the nerve to do the same thing last week. That means he won't stop until he finds me."

Ben's mind raced through the implications. The man was probably trying to protect what he was really doing with that app. He instinctually moved closer on the couch toward her. She didn't flinch, but he didn't touch her. He just wanted his presence to be there, hopefully to offer comfort.

"Kat," he said quietly. She looked up at him, the unshed tears spilling freely now. The sight tore at his heart. "Here's what we're going to do." Ben shifted to face her fully. "First, you're not alone anymore. Whatever happens next, you have someone who knows the truth. Someone who believes you."

She wiped at her tears with her hands.

"Second, I'm going to call Detective Jenna Cole. See what she can tell me about Julian Cross, LifeTrack, and if there are any complaints or investigations."

Hope flickered across Kat's face. "I didn't think about that. You think other people could have experienced what I was going through?"

"It's possible. There's definitely something going on with an app able to track you after you delete it. It must be installing something else as a backdoor on your phone, essentially like a hacker." Ben thought for a moment. "Third, we're going to be smart about this. You stay in Beaufort for now. Keep working at Sweetgrass. Don't change your routine."

She frowned, "You want me to just... wait?"

"I want you to live your life while I figure out our next move. You've been running scared for months. Let me do some of the work now." He reached out, almost touching her hand, then stopped. "I won't let him find you. And if there's a way to stop him, we're going to find it."

Kat stared at him for a long moment. Then slowly, carefully, she reached across the space between them and took his hand. "Why are you helping me?"

Ben thought about Theo. About the case that had killed his partner. He'd spent three years wallowing in his survivor's guilt.

"Because I know what it's like to feel helpless against something bigger than you," he said. He wanted to tell her what Jenna had revealed to him about the connection between the case he'd been investigating and one of LifeTrack's investors. But Kat didn't need to know that now, and it was a part of an official investigation.

His fingers tightened around hers. "It will be okay."

He would share with Jenna about the technology angle. It's quite possible trafficking networks in Atlanta had used apps like LifeTrack to monitor potential victims. He didn't know how involved Julian Cross could be in the trafficking ring. Maybe he'd been using the app as his own personal toy. Either way, Kat had been smart to erase as much of her digital footprint as she could.

Ben would do his best to protect Katrina Bowen.

And find out who killed Theo.

Chapter 22

Beaufort, South Carolina
Wednesday, June 24 at 7:15 a.m.

Katrina woke to sunlight streaming through the curtains of her new bedroom. Though exhausted after sharing her story with Ben, she'd felt it was imperative to have more coverage on her window than the blinds. And the curtains made her bedroom feel almost complete. Katrina still needed to purchase a dresser, but for now she'd been able to hang up her clothes in the closet. She'd stuffed her underwear and socks into a plastic storage unit she found at Dollar General.

She stared at the bare walls. By the weekend, she would hang the rest of the canvases. It felt different listening to the quiet versus hearing the steps of the bed-and-breakfast patrons and smelling Edna's cooking. That she would miss. Luckily, with her still working there, she'd still get to enjoy some meals.

Edna had given her a few days off to get settled. Katrina would return to work on Thursday afternoon in time to help prep for the weekend guests.

She stretched under the sheet, surprised to realize she'd slept through the night. No nightmares. No jerking awake at every sound. Just deep, dreamless sleep.

Maybe it was the exhaustion of setting up her new place.

Or maybe it was the relief of finally telling Ben everything.

She sat up with a thought.

To Edna, Tracey and Jayden, she'd been Kat Miles. Now what? The only other person in town besides Ben who knew her true name was the realtor. Unfortunately, with her given name on the cashier's check, she had to reveal her identity to sign the lease agreement.

How long can I keep hiding who I am?

Katrina padded to the bathroom and splashed water on her face. Then she stared at her reflection in the mirror. It was her, but she felt so far away from the woman who used to film herself doing makeup tutorials and home decor reveals.

She knew Ben would reach out to get intel on Julian and the LifeTrack app, but how long would that take? Over the weekend, she'd started monitoring Julian with her fake account. Since moving into the rental, she hadn't checked in.

By eight o'clock, Katrina had dressed and headed out the door. She'd looked up the closest place to buy a laptop and drove to the Walmart in Bluffton, which was about twenty minutes away. Determined to protect the little place and town she considered her new home, she resolved to handle major errands elsewhere.

Inside Walmart, she made her way to the electronics section. A young man with square shaped glasses approached. "Looking for anything specific?" She estimated the sales associate might have been twenty-two.

"I want to buy a Chromebook," Katrina said. Though she missed her MacBook, she didn't need anything fancy right now. Just something for browsing and basic work.

"We've got a few good options in the three to four hundred dollar range." He led her to a display. "This one's popular. Good battery life, decent speed."

Katrina barely listened to his pitch. She just needed something that worked. Something she could use to get online without creating too much of a digital footprint. Chromebooks were lightweight, secure, harder to track than the operating systems.

She pointed at a mid-range model. "I'll take this one."

The electronic section had its own cash register, so she took out a prepaid Visa card she'd purchased with cash. She wasn't comfortable walking around with too much cash and had grown used to cards. She was almost to the exit with her purchase, when a voice called her name.

Katrina paused, confused. Had she heard her name?

"Katrina? Well, what a surprise!"

Her stomach dropped. She turned to find Michelle Carver standing there, looking every bit the polished professional in white capris and a coral blouse and a designer bag hanging off her arm. The realtor looked out of place, like someone who didn't even shop at a Walmart.

"Michelle." Katrina forced a smile. "Hi."

"Getting settled already?" Michelle's gaze dropped to the bag in Katrina's hand. "I love that you're making the cottage your own. How's everything going? Any issues with the place?"

"No, everything's great. Really comfortable."

"Good, good." Michelle stepped closer, her eyes narrowed slightly as she studied Katrina's face. "You know, when I saw 'Katrina Bowen' on your cashier's check Sunday, the name seemed familiar. But I couldn't place it." She paused, tilting her head. "Then this morning it hit me. You're KatsGlowUp, aren't you? The influencer?"

Katrina's heart pounded.

Michelle's eyes widened with excitement. "I follow you! Your makeup tutorials were amazing. And those locs you had were gorgeous." She stepped back, placing her hand under her chin. "Obviously your hair is completely different now, which is why I didn't recognize you at first. But the bone structure, the eyes..."

The large store suddenly felt too small. Katrina wanted to turn around and run out of the store.

Michelle's smile widened. "Wait, is it actually you? Oh my God, it is, isn't it? I knew it!" She lowered her voice, leaning in. "Are you doing some kind of undercover series? A 'real life' thing? Because I have to tell you, Beaufort would be perfect for that. Very authentic. Small-town Southern charm."

"Michelle." Katrina glanced around, making sure no one else was listening. "Please. I need you not to say anything about this."

The realtor's expression shifted, curiosity replacing excitement. "Oh. Are you...taking a break or something?"

"Something like that." Katrina bounced from one foot to the other, desperate for this conversation to end. "I'm just trying to keep a low profile right now. It's personal. And please...call me Kat, not Katrina."

"Of course, of course." Michelle touched her arm, her voice dropping to a whisper. "I totally understand. Everyone needs privacy sometimes. Your secret's safe with me."

But even as she said it, Katrina could see the speculation in Michelle's eyes. The questions forming.

"Thank you," Katrina said as she walked away. She could feel the woman's eyes on her. The woman said her secret was safe, but could Katrina really trust someone who was clearly dying to know more?

Michelle had been obvious about wanting Ben, but he'd ignored her advances. And Ben had been by Katrina's side, becoming the knight in shining armor she needed. Wanted? Last night felt comfortable, and she could never spill her secrets without the assurance that she could trust Ben.

The moment Katrina was through the doors and into the parking lot, panic set in. She fumbled with her car keys, nearly dropping them before getting the door unlocked. Inside the car, she gripped the steering wheel and forced herself to breathe.

Michelle Carver had recognized her. And if Michelle could recognize her, who else could?

Chapter 23

Lady's Island, South Carolina
Wednesday, June 24 at 7:30 a.m.

Ben stood out on his back porch sipping on black coffee from a mug that had seen better days. He'd been unable to sleep. He wasn't a cop anymore. So why was he acting and thinking like one?

The conversation with Jenna hadn't helped.

"Does she have proof?" Jenna questioned. "I can see why she would've been paranoid about him tracking her, but the man is a tech guru. Suppose it had nothing to do with the app?"

Ben blew out a breath. "So he's just what, testing some technology on her? What about the connection you found to the investor? Back then, while on the case, we were trying to figure out how they were entrapping women inside the trafficking ring."

Jenna stated, "I agree with you. The app is the perfect mechanism. Sounds like it had been in beta for a long time before they officially launched it last year. Who knows how they tested it? We just need evidence before we can go after a tech millionaire. You know this, Ben."

"I know. I know. I don't think Kat has anymore to add. She got rid of everything, including the phone."

Jenna sighed. "Well, maybe there's something she will remember. You said she didn't delete her accounts. There may be an email, a DM, or a text. Something."

Ben didn't make any promises to Jenna. In fact, her request had made him uncomfortable. He liked Kat. Like really liked her. From what she'd told him, the woman was much stronger than she realized. Kat had the smarts to protect herself from a powerful person. Now Jenna wanted Kat to come up with some evidence that would really put her in harm's way.

The cop side of him, the part that loved to close cases, understood.

But the protector side, the one who'd ... developed feelings? He cared about Kat. Even after only knowing her for three weeks, and that was clouding his judgment.

Without any local yards to do, he took a trip out to Lady's Island. He needed someone to run things by, and he wasn't sure when Kat would reveal her identity to Edna, so the bed-and-breakfast owner wasn't the best person to turn to for advice.

Today would have to be Uncle Vern, a fellow cop and family. That was the perspective he needed.

Ben found his uncle and aunt finishing up breakfast. Della offered him a plate. Ben declined but accepted a cup of coffee, which he probably didn't need, since he was already wired.

Uncle Vern gestured, "Let's head out to the porch."

Ben followed his uncle outside. He took a rocker after his uncle eased into one, holding a thermos of coffee.

"What's on your mind this morning, Ben?"

Ben leaned back in the rocker. "A lot, actually."

"How'd that call go with Theo's boy?" Vern asked, his eyes studying Ben's face.

Ben felt a small smile tug at his lips despite everything. "Better than I expected. We talked for about twenty minutes."

"Good. That's real good." Vern nodded slowly. "That boy needed to hear from you. And I suspect you needed to talk to him too."

"I did." Ben took a sip of coffee. "Felt like I put down something heavy I'd been carrying."

"Now, what else is weighing on you? Cause I can tell there's more."

Ben told his uncle everything. About Kat showing up at Sweetgrass three weeks ago, about Julian Cross, and the LifeTrack app. The connection to the shell company he and Theo had been investigating before Theo got shot.

Vern took a swig from his thermos. "That's quite a lot, son. What do you want to do about it? I can see you're chomping at the bit."

Ben rubbed his hand over his head. "I told her I'd help. I don't want her to go through this alone anymore. The situation is bigger than she realizes. Jenna wants me to dig deeper for evidence. But I don't think Kat can help her."

Vern rocked slowly, the chair creaking. "You like this girl."

"What?" His uncle had thrown him a curveball.

His uncle chuckled, "You heard me, Benjamin Wyatt."

Ben shook his head. "Doesn't matter what I feel."

"You care about this woman," Vern continued. "That's not a bad thing. But it's also clouding your judgment."

"No—"

"Let me finish." Vern held up a hand. "When you care about someone, you think with your heart instead of your head. And that's dangerous. For both of you. You know this from being a former cop."

Ben stared at his uncle. "You think I should keep interrogating Kat to see what else she knows? That somehow doesn't seem fair."

"Okay, let's look at this in a different way. Jenna is doing her thing in Atlanta. She needs evidence. Suppose this Julian Cross makes his way here. What will you do? How are you going to be prepared for him?"

Ben could see where his uncle was taking this. Working in the sheriff's office for so many years, his uncle would have a different perspective. What if Kat brings the danger here? It wasn't like Ben hadn't thought about this scenario. Either way, Kat was in more danger than she understood.

His uncle looked out over the yard. "If I was you, I would find out everything I could about this Cross fellow. From public records. Business filings. Any complaints. Lawsuits. The man's in tech, and he has more money than either of us would ever see. He probably didn't come this far without having some dirt on him."

"I agree."

"Ben, you can help her. But you cannot be her protector, her savior, her knight riding in to fix everything." Vern's voice was firm. "That's not fair to her, and it's not fair to you. She needs to be part of whatever solution you come up with. Not a victim you're rescuing."

The truth of his uncle's words stung.

"You left Atlanta because you couldn't save Theo," Vern said quietly. "Because you felt responsible for something that wasn't your fault. Don't make this about trying to prove you can save someone this time."

Ben's throat tightened. "That's not what this is."

"Isn't it?"

The question hung between them. Ben wanted to argue, to insist he was just doing the right thing. But Uncle Vern had a way of cutting through the bull.

"Maybe partly," Ben admitted.

"Then you need to check yourself before you go any further." Vern pointed a callused finger at him. "Because if you're doing this to fix your own guilt, you're not actually helping her. You're using her to feel better about Theo."

The words hit like a punch to the gut.

"Now," Vern continued, "if you genuinely care about this woman, then you bring in professionals. Don't go rogue trying to handle Julian Cross by yourself."

"I wouldn't—"

Vern gave him a look. "I will ask again. What if this man comes here?"

Ben's mind flickered to something Kat had said. "He had her sign contracts," Ben said slowly. "To promote the app."

Vern looked thoughtful. "So there's legal documentation of their business relationship."

"When she brought up the misuse of the app, he wanted to sue her."

"Maybe there's something in that contract he did wrong. Something that would expose what he was really doing."

"She needs a lawyer," Ben said. "I did some contracts with Emmett Craig for my business. Maybe he can take a look."

"It wouldn't hurt to have some legal advice." Vern studied him. "Now, what are you going to do about the *other* matter? The matter of your heart. I can see this woman is under your skin in a different way."

Ben didn't answer at first. His family had always teased him about when he planned to find a woman to settle down with. He was still getting to know Kat, but something must have been obvious to his uncle. He could tell Ben had developed feelings.

"She just escaped a man who manipulated and controlled her," Ben said. "Last thing she needs is me confusing the situation."

"Well, you keep your head on straight. Maybe after y'all sort this mess out, something else can happen. But right now?" Vern eyed him. "Right now, you focus on keeping her safe and getting her the resources she needs. Not on being her hero."

They sat in silence for a while, the June sun growing warm as the rays traveled across the porch.

Uncle Vern had touched a nerve. Another reason Ben had been up last night. He wanted to find Julian Cross and make him answer for what he'd done to Kat. He also needed closure on Theo's death.

He needed to know who was responsible.

Chapter 24

Beaufort, South Carolina
Wednesday, June 24 at 9:00 p.m.

Katrina tried not to worry about her run-in with Michelle at Walmart and concentrated on setting up the Chromebook. She'd made the kitchen table an office space for now until she could find something else for her bedroom. Using her newly created Google account, LittleBird2000, she'd gotten setup in no time. Being a Chrome browser user, the setup was easy. She still missed her MacBook, but this would do.

Her fingers hovered over the keyboard for a few moments while she tried to gather her thoughts. She hadn't looked at her @KatsGlowUp accounts since she'd deactivated them in early May. Seven weeks of silence while her followers wondered what happened to her. What if she took a peek? Could she do that without making her presence visible? Yes, she could browse privately.

Making sure she selected an incognito window, Katrina navigated to Instagram. Her heart pounded as she typed in her username and password.

The screen loaded. And there it was. Her profile. Frozen in time.

@KatsGlowUp Home & Beauty | DIY Queen | Making You and Your Space Glow 89K followers

The profile picture was a different version of her. Her now non-existent honey blonde locs were pulled up high on her head. She'd opted to wear natural makeup. Transparent foundation with just a hint of blush and her favorite mocha lipstick. Behind her smile, she'd already noticed Julian's strange behavior, unable to ignore it. But she hadn't yet understood what she'd gotten herself into becoming a brand ambassador for LifeTrack.

Her last post was on May 3rd. A carousel of photos showing her trip to Dollar Tree. The caption read: *Look what I found at the Dollar Tree. These products are the* SAME *as those name brand products you spend tons of money on. Stay tuned! I'll be sharing my findings.*

Thirteen hundred likes. Four hundred and fifty-two comments. That was way more than she usually got for this type of post. Katrina scrolled through them, her throat tightening with each one. These were her loyal followers. Some of them had even become friends, some content creators she'd met in person.

@BudgetBeautyBabe: *What did you buy at the Dollar Tree? You haven't posted your comparisons.*

@JetSetJess: *Where did you go? Haven't seen you post in forever!*

@GlossAndGlow: *Kat, are you okay?*

@Polished_Perspective: *Miss your content! Hope everything is alright.*

@LipstickLover92: *Did something happen? You just disappeared.*

@TheSkincareSisterhood: *Come back! We need more content from you!*

The comments went on and on. Some from three weeks ago. Some from two weeks ago. Some from just yesterday. She was touched that people had even noticed she'd been missing in action.

Katrina kept scrolling through her feed. For most of the year, she'd been more into decorating the apartment and sporadically posted a makeup reel every few weeks. There were reels of her creating an accent wall without damaging the walls. She really enjoyed how the checkerboard pattern in that project turned out. Too bad she had to take it all apart.

She clicked on one of the few GRWM reels she'd done this year. Those were hard to film because it took most of the day setting up the camera, filming herself in various situations and then moving to the next locations. The Get Ready With Me reel in March highlighted her morning routine. The video opened with her in pajamas with her locs hidden under a huge pink silk bonnet.

"Good morning, beauties! Ready to glow up!" Katrina cringed at how overly bright her voice sounded. "Let's get ready together. I've got a brand meeting later, so we're going full glam today." The video cut to her at her vanity, applying foundation.

Katrina's eyes burned.

I was living my life!

She clicked off the video and navigated to her direct messages. Hundreds of unread DMs. More of the same, followers checking in. Katrina's heart dropped as she recognized some brands reaching out to her.

@VibeStyle_Official *Hey, Kat! We loved working with you on the spring campaign. Any interest in partnering for summer? Let us know.*

@HavenHomeCollective: *Hi! I'm a PR rep with Haven Home. We'd love to send you some pieces to feature. Are you still active?*

@LifeWithLauren: *Hey, Girl. Where are you? I just wanted to make sure you're doing okay. Your content always brightens my day. I miss seeing you!*

This was so depressing. These lost opportunities. Katrina started to click away, but then a familiar name caught her attention, giving her the chills.

Julian!

He rarely reached out in a DM. But of course she'd given him no choice, getting rid of her phone. The data plan. The whole account.

She took a deep breath before clicking on his message, grateful she'd always kept read receipts turned off. At least he wouldn't know she'd looked.

@LifeTrackCEO: *Katrina, we need to talk. You can't just walk away from our agreement. I've invested significant resources in LifeTrack and you committed to being a part of it. Let's meet and discuss this like adults. I'm sure we can work something out.*

There were more messages after that, but she skipped them, scrolling down to the last one. The most recent one, posted just last week.

@LifeTrackCEO: *I will find you, Katrina. You better not do anything stupid or I will destroy you.*

Katrina quickly shut the app. Her hands shook, but not from fear. Rage.

"How dare you! You've messed with me enough, Julian Cross!"

Katrina wasn't big on regrets, but she wished her path had never crossed with that man. Julian had invaded her life like a pest. She was five hours away from the only family she had. And she couldn't reach out to the friends and followers who cared about her. Not to mention six solid years of developing her brand was going to waste, potential opportunities just slipping away.

Anger flared in her chest, hot and sharp.

She missed @KatsGlowUp. Missed the routine of filming and editing. Missed engaging with her followers in the comments. Missed finding a great deal at a thrift store and knowing she could share it with people who'd appreciate it.

Knowing she couldn't risk leaving any trace, Katrina logged out of @KatsGlowUp and sat back in her chair, staring at the blank login screen.

She would not let *him* win.

Then she remembered she needed to be monitoring Julian. She opened a new incognito browser window and navigated to Instagram again. This time, she logged into @littlebird2000.

@LifeTrackCEO was already listed from her last search. The first thing she noticed was a new post since last Saturday.

It was a photo of Julian standing on a waterfront.

@LifeTrackCEO: Sometimes you need to get out of the city to gain perspective. Beautiful day in coastal Georgia. #Savannah #Entrepreneur #Inspiration

Katrina's breath caught in her throat.

He'd posted this photo on Monday. Two days after she'd gone to Savannah to do her banking.

She pushed out of the kitchen chair and almost sent it tumbling to the linoleum floor. "There's no way that's a coincidence."

What if Julian had already been in Savannah? What if he'd seen her?

She ran to the window, peering out at the dark, quiet street. Everything looked normal. Peaceful.

Lord, how do I make him stop?

She didn't know how or what Julian was doing to track her while she was in Savannah. Whatever it was, she knew it was illegal. Just like the LifeTrack app.

She turned back to the laptop, staring at Julian's smug face looking as if he was just out sightseeing in the historical city.

Katrina knew she couldn't keep living like this.

What if, instead of waiting for Julian to find her, she made him come to her? On her terms. She could draw him out.

And then what? Was she really thinking about making herself bait?

Katrina started cackling out loud. Julian had finally driven her over the edge.

No. No, she was perfectly fine. But she had to do something.

Because I'm getting my life back.

Chapter 25

Beaufort, South Carolina
Thursday, June 25 at 10:15 a.m.

Troublesome thoughts plagued Ben as he pulled into Kat's driveway. It pleased him more than he wanted to admit hearing from her this morning. But when she started talking about how she had an idea to run by him, he worried, especially when she claimed it was best to talk in-person. Ben cut the engine and sat for a moment, his instincts on alert. He hoped Kat wasn't thinking about confronting Julian Cross herself. Interesting enough, that was the advice his uncle gave him yesterday.

Ben had experienced dealing with men like Cross. Kat needed to remember there was a reason she felt compelled to run.

Before he could even open the truck door, Kat opened the front door. He could see the determination in her eyes. It kind of thrilled and scared him at the same time. Something had changed in her demeanor. She wasn't the same woman who showed up at the Sweetgrass a few weeks ago.

"Ben," she greeted him as he stepped up on the porch. "Thank you for coming."

"No problem."

She peeked out, eyes darting around him. "Julian is close."

Ben's entire body tensed. He looked up and down the street. "You saw him? Here?"

Kat reached for him, grabbing his arm. "No." She pulled him inside and closed the door. She looked up at him with her solemn brown eyes. "I meant to say he was in Savannah yesterday."

He shook his head. "How do you know this?"

"I will show you. Do you want something to drink? Sweet tea? Water?" she asked, moving toward the kitchen.

His mind was spinning, trying to keep up with her. "Water's fine."

She pulled two bottles from the refrigerator and handed him one.

"Let's sit." Kat took a seat at the kitchen table in front of a laptop.

He settled into the chair next to hers so he could see the screen.

"Remember, I went to Savannah this past Saturday?"

He nodded, urging her to continue.

"I needed to access my bank account. To do it away from Beaufort, somewhere Julian might think I actually was if he's tracking me."

Once again, Kat's strategic thinking impressed him.

She pointed to the screen to what he recognized to be the desktop version of Instagram. He frowned, noting that Kat had been looking at @LifeTrackCEO's account.

He raised an eyebrow. "So, you're tracking him now?"

"Yes, but with a different account. I created a new one."

He peered down at the most recent photo. "He took this selfie in Savannah."

She pointed to the tags in the caption and the location pin. "This may be a coincidence, but you're a former cop. What do you think?"

He sat back. "It's a mighty big coincidence."

Ben frowned, his detective instincts kicking in. "Wait. You said you accessed your bank account in Savannah. You used your real name on the cashier's check?"

Kat nodded. "I had to. Carver Realty needed it for the lease."

"Well, he must have followed your breadcrumbs." Ben's expression darkened. "If you logged into your bank online. That's one ping. Walking inside the bank to show your Real ID, and sign for a cashier's check under Katrina Bowen, his monitoring software would've lit up like a Christmas tree. IP address, geographic location, transaction records. Everything pointed to Savannah."

"Exactly! He's got all these resources, all this technology tracking my every move. And he's harassing my aunt now? That's my last straw. I have a plan."

Warning bells went off in Ben's head. "What kind of plan?"

"Julian thinks he's hunting me, but I can use that. I can control the narrative, choose when and where he finds me."

Ben's stomach dropped. "Wait. What are you saying?"

"I'm saying I want to draw him out. Use myself as bait. But on my terms, in a controlled situation where we—"

"No." Ben stood abruptly. "Absolutely not."

Kat stood too, meeting his eyes. "It's not your decision."

"You're talking about putting yourself directly in the path of a dangerous man—"

"I'm already in his path!" Her voice rose. "Don't you understand? He's in Savannah. That's forty-five minutes from here. He's getting closer. The only question is whether I wait for him to find me, or I take back control."

Ben walked away into her living room, rubbing his hands across his head. This was what Jenna wanted. In fact, if he was still a cop, it was something he would propose. But he wasn't a cop anymore and this woman... No. He couldn't let her do this.

He spun around. "You don't understand what you're dealing with. This guy is connected to—" He stopped himself, almost revealing what Jenna had told him about LifeTrack and Theo's case.

"Connected to what?" Kat demanded. "You know something?"

"To a whole operation that goes well beyond him stalking you." He reached for her, but stopped himself. "What happens if this plan goes wrong?"

"Then at least I tried." She crossed her arms. "At least I fought back instead of spending the rest of my life looking over my shoulder." She pointed a finger at him. "And you said I wasn't alone. Ben, I can do this with your help."

His chest constricted. The fear underneath his anger surfaced, raw and immediate. "I've lost people already. I'm not losing—" He stopped, catching himself.

The silence hung heavy between them.

He sat down on the couch. His Uncle Vern's voice was inside his head.

Kat sat beside him. "Ben?"

Should he tell her?

That LifeTrack App might be involved in a whole human trafficking ring. He was acutely aware of her proximity. She smelled like lavender and vanilla. Up close, he could see how beautiful her skin was. Of course that would be the case with her being a beauty influencer. But she'd walked away from all that.

All because of this man.

A man she wanted to go after her.

He sighed. "We do this together. We do it smart."

She reached over and hugged him. "Thank you."

He froze for a second, stunned that her arms were around him. Slowly, he reached out and put his arm around hers.

She looked at him, their noses almost touching.

“Where do we start?” She asked softly.

He bit his lip. “I need to reach out to Detective Cole. I’m not a cop anymore, Kat.” He smiled. “I can’t just make a citizen’s arrest.”

She pulled away and gave a low chuckle. “Of course. You need backup.”

He grinned back. “Yes, I do.” Then he turned serious. “Kat, this is bigger than just stalking. If Julian’s using that app the way you say, if he’s tracking people without consent, harvesting data—that’s federal.”

She twisted her hands together. “Like the FBI?”

“Probably. But I’m calling Jenna. Detective Cole. She will need to let the Beaufort PD know what’s going on. She can’t just walk into another jurisdiction. And it’s possible this can become a whole sting operation to include the FBI.”

Kat leaned back on the couch, hugging a throw pillow to her body. “Wow. This really is a big deal.”

“You need to be prepared. If you bring this guy down, it’s going to be a big deal.”

“I’ll be ready.” She grabbed his hand. “Thank you, Ben. For not trying to stop me.”

He squeezed her hand back. “I’m not happy about this. But I don’t have any better ideas. You deserve to get your life back.”

Their eyes met and held.

"I should go. Just don't do anything on that computer or phone to draw attention to yourself until I get Detective Cole here. We need a solid plan."

She nodded.

He stepped out into the humid June heat. The door closed behind him with a soft click. Ben climbed into his truck, started it, and waited for the cool air to blow. He pulled away from the curb, feeling a heavy weight on his shoulders. In his rearview mirror, he could see Kat's house growing smaller.

Nothing could go wrong with this crazy plan. He still hadn't told Kat, bringing Julian Cross down could lead to the person responsible for killing Theo.

Please, God, keep Kat safe.

Chapter 26

Sweetgrass Bed and Breakfast
Thursday, June 25 at 4:00 p.m.

Katrina had just finished checking in an older couple returning to the Sweetgrass for the third summer in a row. The woman reminded her a bit of Aunt Lola with her salt and pepper hair. She even threw her head back and laughed like her aunt. Married for thirty years, the husband looked as smitten with his wife as he probably did on their wedding day. Katrina couldn't help but smile as they giggled like two teenagers.

Tracey appeared in the doorway, concern etched across her face. She quickly smiled and greeted the couple. "Mr. and Mrs. Samuels, it's so good to see you back."

Mrs. Samuels gushed. "Oh, this is the highlight of our summer. We love coming back here."

"I love the cooking. Something smells good right now." Mr. Samuels added.

Tracey laughed. “Aunt Edna has been cooking up a storm. Dinner will be at six.”

Mrs. Samuels waved as the couple headed off to their room. “Sounds good. Gives us time to rest and freshen up.”

Tracey walked over to the counter. “Hey, Kat, how’s things going?”

“Everything is good.” She looked at Tracey. The concern Katrina noticed on Tracey’s face a few moments ago had reappeared. “What’s wrong?”

Tracey looked around and stepped closer to Katrina. She held up her phone. “I need to show you something.”

Katrina’s body went still, already sensing that she might not like what Tracey was about to show her.

“I was scrolling through the Beaufort Chamber of Commerce Facebook group during my lunch break, and I saw this post from Michelle Carver.”

Katrina suddenly felt unsteady. She placed her hand on the counter.

@MichelleCarver: A *very special resident started renting a house with Carver Realty and Property Management. Can’t say too much, but let’s just say she’s brought some star power to the Lowcountry.*

There were dozens of comments of people speculating, asking questions, and someone asked if it was a celebrity. Michelle responded she couldn’t reveal details because of client confidentiality.

Katrina’s vision blurred at the edges.

Client confidentiality! Then why did she even bring it up?

"Kat?" Tracey's voice seemed to come from far away. "Are you okay?"

She forced herself to breathe. In through her nose, out through her mouth. She knew it. She felt it in her gut that day at Walmart when Michelle recognized her. This was why she needed to stop this charade. Stop hiding her real identity.

"I'm okay," she managed. She handed the phone back to Tracey. "I just... I need to sit down for a minute."

Tracey guided her to the chairs in front of the bay window.

Katrina focused on the flowers outside the window.

"Talk to me. What's going on?"

Katrina looked over at Tracey. Edna and Tracey had been so kind to her. All this time, she'd been keeping a secret. They deserved the truth.

"I need to tell you and Edna something. Maybe we can do that tonight after dinner."

Tracey didn't press for details, but simply nodded. "Of course. We're having baked chicken tonight. Why don't you invite Ben too? I have a feeling you might want him here."

Katrina's eyebrows shot up.

Tracey teased. "Aunt Edna and I noticed that he's kind of sweet on you. We think you might like him back. Lord knows there haven't been any other women to get that man's attention."

Katrina smiled, forgetting her guilt for a minute. "Really?" Then she remembered what she needed to reveal later tonight.

"Kat?" Tracey leaned over. "Whatever it is, we're here for you. You know that, right?"

Katrina could only nod, her throat felt like it would close up.

"I need to go. Jayden will be back from playing at a friend's house soon."

Katrina let her shoulders drop and let out a long sigh. She took Tracey's advice and texted Ben.

Katrina: *Can you come to dinner at the B&B tonight? I'm telling Edna and Tracey everything. I need you there.*

Ben: *Of course. You've got this.*

She stared at those three words.

You've got this. Did she?

She was about to tell the two women she cared deeply about that she'd been lying to them. Her secret was slowly unraveling.

It will all be over soon. She prayed.

Thursday, June 25 at 6:40 p.m.

Katrina was sure Tracey relayed her request for a conversation after dinner. Edna insisted on moving the feast to the larger dining room, which seated eight. Between the Samuels and Jayden, Katrina didn't have to worry about adding too much to the conversation. Ben sat beside her and across from him was Tracey's boyfriend, Emmett Craig. Katrina had heard about the lawyer, but this was her first time meeting the ginger-haired man. Katrina slid a glance at Ben. The only feature he and Emmett Craig shared in common were their sculpted beards. As if Ben could sense her, he returned her gaze. She couldn't help but blush before turning her attention back to the lovely couple. Katrina could tell Tracey and Emmett were enthralled with each other. She always enjoyed seeing couples truly in love.

She tried to zone back into the conversation but caught Edna's eyes. Something about the way Edna eyed her made Katrina nervous. Though the woman's eyes were warm and inviting, Katrina feared she would disappoint Edna.

I hope they understand why I couldn't reveal my real identity.

Edna pushed back from the dining table. "All right. Everyone full?"

There was a chorus of nods and murmurs.

Mrs. Samuels commented, "This is why I enjoy coming here. Guaranteed to get a good meal. I appreciate your hospitality, Edna, but it's been a long day. Me and Arnold are going to retire for the night. These old bones need some rest.

Edna laughed, "I hear you."

After the older couple went upstairs, Katrina and Tracey helped gather the plates and loaded the dishwasher.

Edna called out as she shuffled forward. "Everyone can meet in our family room."

Tracey nodded. "See you in a minute, Aunt Edna."

In all her weeks at Sweetgrass, Katrina had never set foot past that door leading to the family quarters. When she peered through the open door, Ben and Emmett were already inside.

Tracey touched her arm and dragged her forward. "Come on. You're family."

She stepped through to the family room. In the distance, she could hear Jayden. Tracey rolled her eyes. "Let me go check on that boy. I will be right back."

Katrina took a moment to study the family room. It was smaller than the bed-and-breakfast's sitting room, warmer and lived-in. A comfortable sofa and chairs faced a stone fireplace, its mantel crowded with framed photographs, some in color, and some black and white. More photographs lined the walls, filled the shelves and end tables.

Katrina's eyes moved from photograph to photograph. A young Edna in a graduation gown. A couple that Katrina guessed was Tracey's parents. She recognized the front porch of Sweetgrass in the background, but it had different chairs. The Boyd family photos made Katrina long for her own family. She carried around the framed images of her parents. And her Aunt Lola was now hours away.

"What a beautiful family," Katrina said, before she could stop herself.

Edna had moved to the sofa and settled into one end, patting the cushion beside her. "Thank you, Kat. Why don't you sit down, chile? Rest your nerves. You're safe in here."

Ben leaned against the wall by the window. Edna gestured for him to come over. "No standing around. We have plenty of seats in here. Come get comfortable, Ben."

Ben looked like a scolded little boy. He sat on the couch on the other side of Katrina. She drew comfort from his presence being so near.

Tracey came back into the room and took a chair across from the couch, and Emmett grabbed the other one.

The room was quiet. There was no chatter from Jayden either.

Edna looked at her. "Take your time, honey."

Katrina blinked and looked down at her hands.

"My nickname is Kat," she began. "My Aunt Lola and friends mainly call me Kat. My real name is Katrina Bowen." She swallowed. "The day I showed up here, a few weeks ago, I was on the run from my former life."

No one moved or said a word. All eyes were on her.

Tracey straightened in the armchair. "What happened?"

Katrina slid a look at Ben. He gave her a nod.

"I should talk a little more about my background. Over the past six years, I have developed an online brand @Kats-GlowUp. I'm what they call an influencer. A lot of brands reach out to me and I feature their products. I built up a lot of followers, got a lot of attention."

Tracey leaned forward. "Wait, you're the Kat from KatsGlowUp? Me and my best friend follow you. Well, we follow your new YouTube channel. You do a lot of bargain shopping. I can't believe all this time I didn't realize it was you."

Katrina ran her hand through her short hair. "I got rid of my locs."

"Oh no." Tracey put her hand over her mouth. "That's right. But why?"

Katrina took a breath, not sure how much to say. "One brand I started working with, I realized there was something not quite right with the… product. I confronted the CEO who I'd been dating. He didn't take it well."

Emmett spoke up. "Did he hurt you? Were the police involved?"

Katrina shook her head. "He didn't physically harm me. But because of his resources, he was able to digitally stalk and harass me. He drove me to paranoia. The only way I could see to get away from him was to just shut everything down."

Edna's hand had moved to her chest. "Oh my goodness. Chile, you have been through it."

Katrina nodded. "I'm really tired of it all. He's been to my aunt's house looking for me. That was my last straw." She turned to Ben. "I reached out to Ben this past weekend. It's also why I needed to move out of Sweetgrass."

Edna rubbed Katrina's arm. "Is your aunt okay? Ben, what happens now? Is this man still going to come after Kat?"

Ben leaned forward. “A former colleague of mine checked on Kat’s aunt. She is fine, and the police are looking out for her. But...” He cast a worried glance at Katrina.

She answered for him, “I’m going to use myself as bait. I’m going to reactivate my social media. Let him know I’m here. When he comes, and he will come, Ben and Detective Cole will be ready for him.

“What?!” Both Edna and Tracey shouted.

Emmett, who’d been listening intently, cut in. “That sounds dangerous. Katrina, you said this man started digitally harassing you because you found something at fault with his product. I’m assuming you signed a contract.”

She nodded. “I did.”

He asked, “Do you still have the user agreement? The terms of service?”

Katrina thought for a minute. “It’s probably in my email. I know I might have broken the contract, but ... ”

Emmett held up his hand. “Don’t worry about that. Would you mind forwarding it to me? It’s possible you had the right to break the contract if you found something wrong or illegal.”

“So, he wouldn’t be able to sue me?” Katrina wrung her hands. “I will look for it and send it to you.”

Ben said, “Thank you, Emmett. That would be really helpful. And don’t worry, we’re making sure Kat is protected.”

Tracey piped up. “And we’ll be here too. Do you have a picture of this man? Shouldn’t we be on alert?”

Edna gave a quick nod. "I agree."

Ben and Katrina exchanged glances. Ben said, "We will make sure you have photos, but you must not engage with this man."

Everyone nodded.

Katrina looked around the room. "Thank you. All of you. You know that day I left my aunt's home and started driving, it felt like God guided me here. My parents, when they were alive, would vacation here in the Lowcountry. I haven't been here since I was a little girl."

Edna tilted her head. "You said your last name is Bowen?"

"Yes, ma'am."

"What's your mother's maiden name?"

"Oh! Miles is actually my mother's family name."

"Oh, I see. And you said your mother grew up around here?"

Katrina straightened her shoulders. "Yes, Mom and my aunt Lola grew up somewhere around here. I remember visiting their mother, my grandmother, when I was much younger. We stopped coming after my grandmother passed away. I think I was ten, maybe."

"Interesting. I'm going to look into a few things."

For a moment, Katrina forgot about her troubles.

Did she have more family in the area? If so, why hadn't Aunt Lola told her?

Chapter 27

Sweetgrass Bed and Breakfast
Friday, June 26 at 8:45 a.m.

Anxiety hovered over Ben's body as he steered the truck down the road toward Sweetgrass. Unable to sleep, he'd been up since dawn, his mind churning through everything that could go wrong. The thought of Kat making herself bait made his chest tight with anxiety. When he pulled into the driveway, he caught sight of Kat sitting in the double rocker he'd built.

That put a smile on his face.

"Morning." He called out as he climbed out of the truck.

Kat waved at him. "Good morning."

Climbing the steps, Ben could tell from the way Kat peered at him with bleary eyes that she hadn't gotten much sleep either.

Did she want to back out of this?

"You mind if I sit here with you?"

Kat dazzled him with a smile, making him feel things he really didn't need to feel this early in the morning.

"Of course."

He slid next to her on the rocker, admiring his work.

Kat patted the arm of the rocker. "I heard this was your handiwork. All these rockers. You're quite talented, Ben."

He blushed. "It's just a hobby I enjoy." To get the attention off him, he asked, "You doing okay?"

Kat sighed, losing her smile. "No. I keep thinking about what I'm about to do, and I'm not sure if it's the right thing or not."

Ben took her hand. "You don't have to do this. We can find another way."

"No, we can't. This is the only way it ends. I know that."

Kat hadn't removed her hand from his, so they sat like that until a dark SUV entered the street.

Ben let go of Kat's hand and stood. His eyes narrowed as the SUV pulled into the Sweetgrass driveway beside his truck. Then he breathed a sigh of release when a woman got out.

Detective Jenna Cole.

She looked the same, but somehow different. Her dark brown hair was pulled back in a ponytail. From the time Ben had known and dated the detective, Jenna had always opted for a short haircut. It surprised him she'd let it grow out. She wore jeans and a blazer. Ben could tell she had her issued piece under the blazer.

While he didn't have a reason to, Ben had taken out his own Glock last night. He didn't want to alarm Kat, but he'd wear it if he needed to.

Ben stepped down to greet Jenna.

She smiled up at him, her hazel eyes sparkling in the sunlight.

"Ben? You look good. Landscaping has done wonders for you." She glanced admiringly at his arm, which had grown more muscular over the past three years. Hard work outside did that for him.

"Thank you for coming all the way from Atlanta."

Jenna's smile turned serious. "This case matters to me." She walked up the porch steps, turning her attention to Kat. "You must be Katrina Bowen."

Kat stood and held out her hand. "Detective Cole."

Jenna shook her hand. "Please, call me Jenna. Thank you for agreeing to meet with me."

Edna showed up at the door. "Ben. You and the ladies come on inside for some breakfast."

Ben turned, startled to hear Edna's voice. "Yes, ma'am."

Jenna raised an eyebrow. "Can't say no to that."

"You're not going to want to. Edna is the best cook around. Her guests come back here just to eat her cooking alone."

When they arrived in the kitchen, Edna had mugs sitting out on the counter along with condiments.

"You must be the detective. I'm Edna Mae Boyd. Welcome to Sweetgrass." She gestured to the kitchen table. "Coffee's fresh. Have a seat. I have some homemade sticky buns coming out of the oven soon."

"Thank you, ma'am, for the hospitality." Jenna commented.

"Not a problem." Edna waved. "After you eat, we'll get you settled in the Blue room upstairs. Kat has it ready for you."

They settled around the table after making their coffee. Kat and Ben took the chairs on one side, and Jenna sat across from them.

Jenna took a sip of her coffee. "Oooh, that's good. Do you all mind if I get started?"

Kat nodded. "Sure." She glanced back at Edna. "Everyone knows why I'm here and what's going to happen."

Edna called out as she headed over with a pan in between her gloved hands. "And we're here to support her and get this man out of her life for good." She sat the piping hot buns covered with white icing in the center of the table. "Ben, can you grab those dishes at the end of the table and pass them around?"

He did as he was told, his mouth watering to take a bite of that goodness.

Everyone grabbed a piece. For a few moments, there was silence as forks stabbed at the buns and slurped coffee.

"Oh my goodness." Jenna shook her head. "Ben, no wonder we can't get you to come back to Atlanta. Miss Edna has you spoiled."

Edna laughed in the background. "I'm sure there are more things about the Lowcountry that keep Ben tied to this place.

There's plenty of coffee in the pot if you need refills. I'm going to head up front so you all can talk business. Let me know if you need anything else."

After Edna exited the kitchen, Jenna pulled a folder from her bag but didn't open it. "Katrina, I want to start by saying I believe everything you've told us about Julian Cross and what he's done to you. I'm going to do everything in my power to help you."

Kat's hands were wrapped around her coffee mug. "Thank you."

"You need to know, I've been investigating LifeTrack for several months now," Jenna continued. "It started with a tip from a tech analyst who noticed unusual data patterns in some of the app's traffic. The more we dug, the more concerned we became."

Ben felt Kat tense beside him. He reached under the table and found her hand lacing his fingers through hers.

Jenna leaned forward slightly. "We believe LifeTrack may have been used to track victims of human trafficking."

Kat's hand tightened on Ben's so hard it hurt.

"What?" Kat's voice was barely a whisper.

"We're not certain yet," Jenna said carefully. "But we've found evidence that suggests the location tracking within the app's technology can monitor someone's movements in real-time."

Ben was concerned with how still Kat had gone. He could feel her hand shaking in his. He reached over with his other hand to rub her hands. "Kat, are you okay?"

"Oh my God." Kat's shoulders shook. "All this time, I thought it was just me. But he was doing this to other women? Using that app to—" She snatched her hands from Ben, covering her face. "I convinced my followers to download it. I promoted it on my platform. What if I helped him hurt people?"

Ben put his hands on her shoulders. "That's not on you. You didn't know."

"But I should have—"

"No." Jenna's voice cut through. "Katrina, look at me."

Kat's eyes were bright with unshed tears.

"You are not responsible for what Julian Cross has done," Jenna said. "He manipulated you. He used your trust, your platform, your relationship. That's on him, not you. Do you understand?"

Kat nodded, but Ben could see she didn't quite believe it.

"We want access to the investors. One, in particular, has come up in another case." Jenna shot a look at Ben.

He gave her a subtle head shake. Ben had chosen to not tell Kat about the connection to Theo. He didn't feel it was appropriate. In fact, now he was wondering if he could have done more on that case. After Theo's death, he'd just let it all go.

Jenna's voice interrupted his thoughts. "Before we can get to the people funding LifeTrack's development, to the source code, the user data, everything, we need probable cause for a warrant. That's where you come in."

"My plan," Kat said.

"Yes. If Julian shows up at your location after tracking you through the app, that gives us what we need. It proves he's been using LifeTrack to stalk you, which opens the door to investigating the app more broadly."

"How many other women might he be tracking right now?" she asked.

"We don't know," Jenna admitted.

"But if we do this, you can find out? You can stop him?"

"We can try. I can't promise anything, but this gives us our best shot."

Kat took a deep breath. "Then we do it."

Ben's stomach dropped. He still didn't like this plan, but what choice did they have?

Jenna pulled out a notepad. "Okay, let's talk through this plan."

"First, I need to buy a new phone," Kat began. "A smartphone I can install LifeTrack on. Then I'll activate my Instagram account. What about if I post a photo that shows I'm in Beaufort?"

Jenna looked at her. "And you think Julian will see it?"

"He was in Savannah a few days after I was there. He was just at my aunt's house before that. And..." Kat opened her Chromebook. "I brought my laptop so I could show you. He sent me a DM."

Ben frowned. “I didn’t know that.”

Kat looked sheepish. “Sorry, I forgot to show you.” She turned the computer screen around.

Ben and Jenna leaned in to read. As soon as Ben saw the message, he got heated.

@LifeTrackCEO: *I will find you, Katrina. You better not do anything stupid or I will destroy you.*

Jenna’s eyes flashed as well. “He’s threatening you. Keep all of that correspondence. We can use that. We’ll need to position officers,” Jenna said, making notes. “Plain clothes, at a distance, so we don’t spook him. I’ll coordinate with the Beaufort PD. And…” Jenna sighed. “I need to bring in the FBI. I’m way out of my jurisdiction, and this app is more of a federal thing.”

Ben, still steaming about the message and the fact Kat hadn’t shown it to him, inserted. “My Uncle Vern can help ease you in. He’s a retired deputy with Beaufort Sheriff’s department.”

“Sounds good. We definitely need to let them know and we’ll need their help.”

They spent the next hour going over details, determining when Kat should post and when the FBI would arrive. Ben listened to all of it, his dread growing. The plan was sound, but that didn’t make him feel any better about it.

Anything could happen.

Chapter 28

Beaufort, South Carolina
Friday, June 26 at 12:08 p.m.

Katrina's hands were still shaking as Ben pulled out of Sweetgrass's driveway. She stared out the passenger window, watching Beaufort's familiar streets blur past, but her mind was miles away. Jenna's words kept echoing in her head.

We believe LifeTrack may have been used to track victims of human trafficking.

How many women? How many people had Julian's app been used to hurt?

And she'd promoted it. Convinced her followers to download it. Used her platform, her trust with her community, to spread his surveillance tool.

The guilt threatened to choke her.

"Hey." Ben's voice cut through her spiral. "You okay?"

She turned to look at him. His hands gripped the steering wheel, jaw tight. He'd been quiet since they left the bed-and-breakfast. "Did you know? I mean, how long have you known?"

He looked at her. "The app? The human trafficking element? Jenna mentioned something to me about a case I'd been working on with my partner. The one that took his life."

Katrina frowned. "LifeTrack is connected?"

Ben knew it was time to come clean with everything. He blew out a breath. "A shell company, Horizon Capital Partner, invested in LifeTrack. It was the same company we were pursuing. Jenna thinks maybe during the beta testing of this app, they may have used it for—"

"Human trafficking." She gritted her teeth. "We have to get him, Ben."

He gazed at her. "Yes, we do. But first, let's get you this iPhone."

They pulled into a strip shopping mall where an AT&T sat next to a Subway. Katrina's stomach churned as they walked through the automatic doors into the bright, overwhelming electronics store. Ten minutes later, Katrina had a brand new iPhone 17 Pro and a newly created data plan. She paid with bills from the envelope she kept hidden in her purse.

Ben didn't say anything, but she was sure he'd seen all the cash. Even now, she still wanted to be careful. The situation with Julian had trained her to be paranoid.

Back in Ben's truck, Katrina held the sleek box in her lap. She hadn't held an iPhone in her hands since early May. Almost two months of living with a burner phone. She'd unboxed dozens of products on videos for her followers. This unboxing held no excitement for her.

She powered on the phone. The Apple logo glowed, welcoming her. Then that familiar setup screen appeared.

Hello.

Katrina swiped through the setup screens with practiced ease. After connecting to her brand new data plan, she logged in with her iCloud account. This was a big step. When the home screen finally appeared, she let out a breath she hadn't realized she'd been holding.

"Okay," she said quietly. "We're getting there. Time to install LifeTrack."

She opened the App Store and typed in the search bar with fingers that wanted to shake: *LifeTrack.*

The app appeared immediately. That sleek blue and white logo Julian had been so proud of. The one she'd featured in countless Instagram stories and posts. The reviews were still glowing. 4.8 stars. Hundreds of thousands of downloads. How many of those people had she convinced to install it?

Katrina pressed download. The app installed quickly. When she opened it, that familiar interface greeted her. The login screen appeared. She stared at it for a long moment. Once she logged in with her old credentials, Julian would know. Maybe not immediately, but soon.

Ben must have noticed her hesitation. "You sure about this?"

Katrina looked at him. Really looked at him. This man who'd somehow become her anchor in just a few weeks. Who'd listened to her story without judgment. Who was here supporting her even though she knew he didn't like the idea of her being bait.

"I'm sure," she said. "If this app has been used to hurt people, I have to do whatever I can to stop it."

She typed in her email address. Then her password. Her fingers hovered over the login button. This was it. No going back after this. She pressed Login.

The app opened to her old dashboard. Everything was exactly as she'd left it in April. Her carefully organized calendar. Her fitness goals. Her journal entries about building her brand and growing her following. A life that felt like it belonged to someone else now.

The location services prompt immediately popped up.

LifeTrack would like to access your location. Allow while using app / Allow once / Don't allow.

Katrina's thumb moved to *Don't Allow.*

Katrina set the phone in her lap and closed her eyes, breathing through a wave of nausea. "I'm logged in," she whispered. "Even though my location isn't on, I'm pretty sure he can see me now."

Ben reached over and took her hand. "He doesn't know where you actually live. Just that you're in Beaufort. We're in control here. He's going to mess up."

She wanted to believe that. Wanted to believe they'd thought of everything.

Alright, Julian, come find me.

Friday, June 26 at 1:52 p.m.

Despite all that was going on, it was a beautiful afternoon. Ben drove them to Henry C. Chambers Waterfront Park. Edna had suggested it would be a great place to take a photo, and Katrina hadn't been here before. Katrina had to smile, wondering if Edna had some intentions of suggesting this place. She saw couples walking along the wooden boardwalk, some on benches overlooking the Beaufort River, where sailboats drifted.

It all felt romantic. And why was her mind even thinking about romance? She was about to become bait.

"Where do you want to do this?" Ben asked.

Grateful for Ben grounding her, Katrina scanned the park. "Over there." She pointed to a spot near the water where the old bridge was visible in the background. They walked to the spot together. Katrina handed Ben her new iPhone, then stood by the railing overlooking the water. The late afternoon sun was perfect. This was the kind of light she used to chase for content.

"How do you want to pose?" Ben asked, looking uncomfortable holding the phone.

Katrina giggled. “I know you’ve used a camera on your phone before. Just take a few candid shots. Make it look natural, like someone caught me in a moment.”

She turned slightly away from the camera, looking out at the water. Katrina did her best to make her shoulders relaxed and tilted her face toward the sun. Years of making content, she knew her perfect angles.

“Okay,” Ben cleared his throat. “I think I got some good ones.”

Katrina walked back to him and took the phone. She swiped through the photos Ben had taken.

She teased. “Great job. We can add photographer to your list of talents.”

Katrina wasn’t kidding. She looked way more peaceful than she felt. Her short hair caught the sunlight. She had to admit the style was growing on her. The locs had weighed her down, and it took a lot of time and energy to keep up with her re-twists. Now her hair was... free.

She looked like a new version of @KatsGlowUp, finding herself again.

Katrina checked the time on her phone. 2:29 p.m. “I’m going to post this before we leave like we planned.”

Ben nodded. “I like that idea. Keep your location in a public place.”

Back in the truck, she downloaded and opened Instagram. Once she logged into @KatsGlowUp, anxiety crept in again. Not because of Julian, but because she’d just left her followers hanging. Even more importantly, she had inadvertently promoted an app that posed a hidden danger.

Katrina uploaded a few of the photos Ben had taken to create a carousel post. Then she typed.

@KatsGlowUp: *Needed some time away. More to come.*

She tagged the location: Beaufort, South Carolina.

Another breadcrumb for Julian to follow. She didn't hesitate this time, publishing the post. She observed Instagram process her post. It took only a minute before notifications started flooding in. Her phone vibrated continuously with notifications. She couldn't enjoy it, nor would she respond right now.

"Bait sent." She stuffed the phone into her bag.

Ben nodded. "Let's get you home and touch base with Jenna."

Now that they'd prepared the trap for Julian, would he come?

Will I be ready to face him?

Friday, June 26 at 4:15 p.m.

The FBI arrived in an unmarked white van that could've belonged to any contractor. Ben watched from Kat's living room window as two agents climbed out, a woman in her mid-thirties with sharp eyes and quick movements, and a tall man who carried himself with the rigid posture of someone who'd spent years in law enforcement.

Jenna made the introductions. "Special Agent Marcus Webb, Special Agent Sarah Kim, this is Ben Wyatt and Katrina Bowen."

Webb's handshake was firm, professional. "Ms. Bowen, we'll do everything we can to keep you safe tonight."

Agent Kim was already moving through the house, tablet in hand. "Let's get the cameras installed."

For the next hour, Ben watched as Kim worked with quiet efficiency, mounting tiny cameras, testing angles, running through the feeds on her tablet. Webb coordinated with Beaufort PD over the phone, his voice clipped and authoritative.

Ben found himself in the kitchen with Webb, who was examining the entry points.

Ben frowned, looking at the back door. "This lock won't hold. I told Kat to get it replaced."

Agent Webb nodded. "We're leaving it that way."

"What?" Ben's voice rose. "You're deliberately—"

"We need him to make entry," Webb interrupted. "It's the logical point of entry. Neighbors won't see him. We will monitor the back door with thermal imaging, cameras, audio. The moment he touches that doorknob, we'll know. The moment it splinters, we move."

Kim appeared in the kitchen doorway. "I've reinforced it slightly with a support brace behind the frame. It'll hold long enough for us to get into position, but not so much that he'll be deterred. We want him to think he's being clever."

Ben glared at them.

"I know you don't like it, but she IS the bait," Webb said flatly. "Monitored bait. We'll be on him in thirty seconds."

"Thirty seconds is a long time for her to be alone with him."

"Which is why we will have all perimeters covered," Webb said. "Close enough to respond, far enough not to spook him. Ms. Bowen has the panic button. The moment she presses it or the moment we see him get aggressive, we're through that door."

Webb moved in closer to him. "I know you're a former Atlanta PD detective, but *this* is an FBI operation now." Webb turned to Jenna. "Detective Cole. Your civilian friend stays in the vehicle. No heroics."

Jenna responded with a tight smile. "Of course."

Ben exchanged a glance with Jenna once Webb turned his back.

He didn't like the feds. And he certainly didn't like this plan.

Chapter 29

Friday, June 26 at 10:47 p.m.

Ben couldn't believe he was sitting in a surveillance vehicle, watching someone he cared about walk into danger. A block north, the FBI had set up their mobile command center in a nondescript white van packed with surveillance equipment and the two special agents Ben had met briefly that afternoon.

The agents weren't happy about Ben being involved. Despite his law enforcement background, he was a civilian now. Ben didn't care. He wasn't leaving Kat alone.

That had been six hours ago. They'd spent the afternoon running through the operation plan, positioning cameras, coordinating with Beaufort PD.

"*Two angles on the living room, one on the kitchen, thermal imaging on the back door*," Kim had said, her fingers flying across her tablet. "*The moment he makes entry, we'll have him on multiple feeds. Audio and visual.*"

Now he sat in Jenna's SUV, two houses down from Kat's house, positioned so they had a clear view of the quiet street. Her laptop showed Kat's living room in grainy night vision. The FBI camera feed was also streaming to local PD.

In the back of his mind, he could hear Uncle Vernon warning him not to be a hero.

He trusted Jenna and the agents, but the woman he'd only known for a few weeks had captivated him. This afternoon's photo shoot to set up the electronic bait had set Ben's heart on fire in ways he couldn't imagine. Despite what was going down, Kat looked beautiful and carefree with the water at her back. This was clearly no time to think about having a future with her, but he couldn't seem to get the images out of his mind.

An earpiece connected Jenna to the FBI's communication channel, where she could hear Webb and Kim coordinating with the Beaufort PD units stationed at the perimeter. Jenna took out the earpiece so he could hear.

"*Command to all units, status check*," Webb's voice crackled through the earpiece.

"*Unit One, north perimeter clear*," a Beaufort deputy responded.

"*Unit Two, south perimeter clear.*"

"*Unit Three, east perimeter clear.*"

Jenna touched her earpiece. "Unit Four, visual on the target residence. Subject appears calm."

On screen, Kat sat curled on the couch, phone in hand, occasionally standing to pace before sitting again. The Instagram post had gone up hours ago. It was nearly eleven at night.

"Maybe he didn't see it," Jenna said quietly, breaking the silence that had settled over them for the past thirty minutes.

Ben's jaw tightened. "He saw it."

"Then maybe he's smarter than we thought. Maybe he knows it's a trap."

Ben gestured to her laptop. "Or maybe he ditched his phone and we have no way of knowing he's coming."

"*Command to Unit Four*," Webb's voice cut through their conversation. "*We're running another sweep of traffic cameras within a fifty-mile radius. If Cross is mobile, we'll pick him up.*"

Jenna pressed her earpiece. "Copy that, Command. Any hits on his vehicle?"

"*Negative. Last confirmed sighting was his Tesla at his Atlanta residence at 1600 hours. Nothing since.*"

"He knows how tracking works," Jenna said. "Cross knows Teslas are trackable. If his vehicle hasn't moved from his Atlanta garage since Monday, then he's using a different car. Probably a rental under a fake name or a burner vehicle."

"*He could already be here*," Agent Kim added over the comms. "*Could've arrived hours ago, watching, waiting for the right moment.*"

Every instinct Ben had screamed at him to go inside, to stay with Kat to not leave her alone. But she'd insisted she had to do this alone. Julian wouldn't come if he saw another car, saw any sign of someone with her.

It felt too much like that night with Theo. They'd split up, going separate ways when they should have stayed together.

This isn't the same. We have backup.

"She's holding up better than I expected," Jenna said, watching Kat check her phone again on the feed.

Ben couldn't take his eyes off the screen. "She's terrified."

"She needs to be scared. It will keep her alert." Jenna glanced at her watch. "But we can't keep her on edge all night. If he doesn't show by midnight—"

"He'll show."

"Ben." Jenna chastised. "We might need to accept that this didn't work. That he's too cautious, or too smart."

His phone buzzed.

Katrina: *Is he coming? It's been almost five hours.*

Ben stared at the message. What could he say? That they didn't know? That Julian had vanished from every tracking system they had? That they might have put her through this terror for nothing?

Ben: *Stay alert. He could still show.*

But even as he sent it, doubt crept in. Maybe Jenna was right. Maybe Julian had seen through the trap.

Friday, June 26 at 11:12 p.m.

Katrina had grown tired. It had been a long day since Detective Cole's arrival. She'd revealed who she was to Edna and her family. Reached out to her followers, only to ignore them again. Her fingers tightened around her phone. She'd been watching the comments flood in on the post she'd published earlier.

But had Julian seen it?

The FBI was here!

Special Agent Kim had been professional but intense, moving through Katrina's house that afternoon to install tiny cameras while explaining each one.

"*One above your TV, angled toward the couch,*" Kim had said, attaching something no bigger than a button to the wall. "*One in the kitchen entrance. Both have audio. We'll have eyes and ears on everything.*"

Katrina had watched, feeling both protected and exposed. "*What if he sees them?*"

"He *won't.*" Kim had pulled out her tablet, showing Katrina the feed. "*These are military-grade. Unless he knows exactly where to look, he'll never spot them.*"

Special Agent Webb, Kim's quite intimidating looking partner, had been less reassuring. Towering over her, the man was even taller than Ben.

"*The moment he makes entry, you move away from him,*" Webb had instructed, his tone left no room for argument. "*Don't engage. Don't confront. Let him talk, let him reveal his intentions. We need him on camera making threats or attempting physical contact.*"

"*And if he grabs me before you can get inside?*" Katrina had asked.

"*That won't happen. We'll be thirty seconds away, maximum.*" Webb had handed her a small device. "*Panic button. You press this, we come in immediately.* No *waiting.*"

Now, hours later, Katrina sat on her couch, the panic button on the coffee table within arm's reach. She could feel the cameras watching her. Katrina glanced up at the tiny camera above her TV, wondering if Ben was watching right now. He wanted to stay inside with her, but she knew she needed to do this alone.

Special Agent Kim and Detective Cole thought Julian was a coward, hiding behind his technology. Julian wouldn't want to face Ben.

She smiled at the picture in her mind.

Katrina walked into the kitchen to put on the teakettle. Her Aunt Lola would suggest she have some chamomile tea to soothe her nerves. She might as well settle down and go to bed, though she doubted she could fall asleep easily. Exhaustion mingled with anxiety, making her feel too jittery to lie down. Reading might do the trick. Focus her mind somewhere else besides her current situation.

She headed to her bathroom to wash her face. The cleansing gel had tea tree oil, which made her face tingle the way she liked it. Katrina splashed her face with water and patted it dry as she looked at her tired eyes in the mirror. *Get some tea and then go to bed.* Katrina headed back into the kitchen just as the teakettle whistled.

She returned to the couch with her cup of tea, but before she could take a sip, a sound startled her. She listened, but didn't hear it again.

She sipped, letting the warm tea slide down her throat into her chest.

Then she froze, hearing the sound again. Slowly, she placed the cup on the coffee table and turned toward the kitchen. Was she hearing things? Ben had told her to stay alert.

The sound came again. Not a scrape this time. A rattle. Like someone testing a doorknob.

Oh no! The back door!

The one Ben had warned her about. The one with just a simple handle lock. She grabbed her phone off the coffee table and frantically started typing.

Katrina: *Someone's at the back door*

Ben: *It's him. Use the panic button.*

A sharp crack split the air. The sound of wood splintering.

The cameras. Agent Kim is watching. The FBI sees this. They're coming.

But how long would it take them to get here? Thirty seconds, Webb had said.

Footsteps. Slow. Deliberate. Moving through her kitchen.

She had to face him.

Katrina stood. She knew she should reach for the panic button, but her hands felt frozen. She contemplated heading down the hallway when Julian stepped into view.

The camera above her TV was recording everything. Ben was watching. The FBI was watching.

But none of them were here.

How long would they really wait?

Friday, June 26 at 11:36 p.m.

Kat: *Someone's at the back door.*

Ice slid down Ben's spine. He wanted to kick himself. The FBI had left that door accessible on purpose, but that didn't make him feel any better about it.

"*I've got thermal confirmation,*" Agent Kim's voice crackled through the earpiece. "*Single person, rear approach. He's at the back door.*"

"*All units, stand by,*" Webb ordered. "*Wait for entry before—*"

A sharp crack split the night air.

"*That's forced entry!*" Kim's voice rose. "*He's inside! He's inside!*"

"*All units* GO! GO! GO!" Webb shouted.

By the time he heard the doors on the FBI van slam open, boots hitting pavement, Ben was already out of Jenna's SUV, running toward Kat's house. He heard Jenna shout behind him to stand down. But all Ben could think about was Katrina, alone in that house with Julian Cross.

Friday, June 26 at 11:38 pm

Even in the dim light, she could tell he looked exactly the same. Dark blond hair perfectly styled. He wore an expensive button-down shirt and designer jeans, like he was heading to a business meeting instead of breaking into someone's home. His green eyes gazed at her like emeralds.

"Hello, Katrina," Julian said calmly. "Nice place you've got here."

Her voice came out steadier than she expected. "You really just broke into my house."

"Your house?" Julian smiled, but it didn't reach his eyes. He spread out his arms. "Katrina, what are you doing here? What have you done to yourself? Your hair?"

"You should not be here. I told you I was done." She squeaked out. "How did you find me?"

Julian took a step forward.

Katrina forced herself not to back up.

"Before me, you were just another beauty influencer. I gave you legitimacy. Money. And this is how you repay me?"

"You stalked me." She gripped her phone, praying the FBI, Jenna... Ben would get here soon. "You tracked me without my consent. You and your LifeTrack app are not as safe as you tout it to be."

Julian laughed. "Katrina, stop talking all of this nonsense."

"If I'm talking nonsense, how did you know how to find me?"

He took another step closer. "I have nothing to hide. I've created a popular app that people love. It keeps everyone connected wherever they are in the world."

"Connected!" Katrina said, anger burning through her fear. "You used my platform to spread your surveillance app. To track people. To hurt people."

He shook his head, making his hair fall over his eye. "What! I've never hurt anyone. I provided a service. Connection. Security. Peace of mind."

"You're crazy!"

Julian's expression darkened. "I don't appreciate you saying that. I'm perfectly sane. And I'm not letting some beauty influencer ruin years of hard work."

He lunged.

Katrina grabbed the lamp she'd found in Sweetgrass's storage and swung with everything she had.

The ceramic base connected with Julian's temple with a sickening crack.

He stumbled, his hand went to his head, blood seeping between his fingers. "You —"

She swung again, but he was faster than she expected. He hit her in the face, stunning her. His hands gripped her arm so tight, she let go of the lamp. She screamed in pain and slapped at his hands. "Let me go."

Julian's grip tightened painfully. "You think you can just—"

The front door exploded inward. Agent Webb, two deputies, and Jenna launched inside, weapons drawn. "FBI! Don't move!"

Julian threw up his hands. A deputy quickly grabbed one of his arms, twisting it behind his back. Another deputy came up and helped wrestle Julian to the ground.

Webb shouted, "Julian Cross, you're under arrest for stalking, breaking and entering, assault, and unlawful surveillance. You have the right to remain..."

Katrina sank against the wall, her legs giving out. She slid to the floor, watching as the deputies cuffed Julian.

Julian was screaming. "This is a mistake. You're making a mistake. I'm Julian Cross."

Katrina wanted to laugh with relief, but her face throbbed.

Ben crossed to Katrina in three long strides. He dropped to his knees beside her. "Are you hurt? Let me look at your face."

Her voice came out shaky. "He got me good, but I hit him with the lamp."

Ben's hands were gentle as he checked her arm where Julian had grabbed her. "You clocked him good."

She let out a shaky laugh. "I was terrified."

"I know. But you stood your ground." He pulled her into his arms, and she let herself collapse against his chest. Let herself shake. Let herself feel everything she'd been holding back.

She pulled back from Ben, wiping at her eyes. "Is it really over?"

"The arrest is just the beginning." Ben cupped her face with his hands. "But, yeah, no more running and hiding for you."

Chapter 30

Sweetgrass Bed & Breakfast
Saturday, June 27 at 7:15 a.m.

Katrina sat up slowly, her body aching. Edna had put her in the Green room for now, since Jenna was using the Blue room. The sage green walls and botanical prints felt more peaceful somehow, more grounding after last night's chaos.

Her face throbbed where Julian had hit her. She touched her cheekbone gingerly, wincing at the tenderness. The bruise would be spectacular by now. The events of last night played through her mind in fragments. Julian in the flesh. Her panic. Her fighting back. The FBI and cops crashing through the door. Julian being dragged out in handcuffs.

She pulled the quilt tighter around her shoulders, grateful to be back at Sweetgrass. Her little rental had become a crime scene. Just after she tried to make it her home.

Her new iPhone sat on the nightstand, the screen dark. She needed to call her aunt Lola before she saw something online. They'd placed Julian in custody last night, but like Ben said, this was just the beginning. It could get a lot worse when people found out.

Katrina took a breath and dialed.

Aunt Lola picked up on the second ring. “Hello?”

Realizing her aunt didn’t have her new phone number, she said, “It’s me, Aunt Lola. I’m okay.”

Her aunt let out a deep sigh. “What happened? Where are you? He was on the news. They arrested Julian Cross.”

Katrina closed her eyes, hating she hadn’t called sooner. But everything happened so fast once the FBI took Julian into custody. She had to pack her bags quickly, and Ben took her to Sweetgrass. Edna had been waiting. It was already almost two in the morning by then.

Katrina croaked. “He found me.”

A sharp intake of breath. “Jesus. Are you hurt?”

“I’m okay. He... he broke into my house last night, but the police were there. The FBI. They arrested him.”

“The FBI? Katrina, where are you right now?”

“I’m in Beaufort. South Carolina. I’ve been here since June.”

There was a long pause. When Lola spoke again, her voice cracked. “You’re in Beaufort?”

“Yeah, I—”

“Baby, that’s where your mama and I grew up. That’s home.”

Katrina felt the world tilt. “When I was looking for somewhere to go, I saw Beaufort and it felt right. I remember Mom and Dad bringing me to the Lowcountry when I was little.”

Lola's voice was soft. "Your mama used to say the Lowcountry always called her back, even when she tried to stay away. Maybe it called you too."

"Maybe so."

"You've been there since June and you didn't tell me?"

Katrina heard the hurt beneath the words. "I couldn't risk anyone knowing where I was. Not even you. Julian was tracking everything."

Lola's voice softened. "I know, baby. I know. I'm just glad you're safe. Your mama would've wanted you there. She always missed it, even though she never went back."

"Why didn't she ever go back?"

"Too many memories. Losing Mama there… it was hard on her. And me. But that doesn't mean it's not a good place." Lola paused. "You being there, that feels right."

"It does feel right. Like I'm supposed to be here."

"Then you stay there. You stay where you feel safe. But you keep me posted, you hear? And when this is all over, I'm coming to visit. I haven't been back in fifteen years. Since Mama died. It's time."

Katrina smiled despite everything. "I'd like that."

"I love you, Katrina."

"I love you too."

After they hung up, Katrina sat with the phone in her hand. Her mother's home.

Maybe her home now.

She had lots of reasons to stay.

Saturday, June 27 at 8:20 a.m.

The kitchen smelled like coffee and bacon. Edna stood at the stove, Tracey was setting the table, and Jayden was coloring at the table. Emmett sat at the table with a briefcase open beside him, papers spread out. Everyone looked up when Katrina appeared in the doorway.

Edna's face softened. "There she is. Come sit down, chile. I've got breakfast ready."

Katrina slid into a chair.

Jayden looked up from his coloring. "Why is your face purple?"

"Jayden," Tracey said gently.

"It's okay." Katrina managed a smile. "I got hurt last night, but I'm okay now."

Jayden frowned, his face concerned. "Someone hurt you?"

Katrina's throat tightened. "Yeah. But the police caught him. He can't hurt anyone anymore."

Jayden looked relieved and went back to his coloring. "Good."

Edna set a plate of eggs, bacon, grits, and toast in front of Katrina. "You need to eat something."

Katrina picked up her fork, though she had no appetite. "I need to call Michelle Carver this morning. About the doors."

Tracey looked up sharply. "You're not thinking about going back there, are you?"

"I paid four months' rent on that house. And I have a lease. I have to go back, eventually."

Edna shook her head. "Eventually, yes. But not today, honey. Not for a while."

Emmett said. "Michelle is a businesswoman. She'll understand about the doors. As a landlord, Michelle's dealt with worse."

"You're staying here until the house is secure," Tracey added. "Non-negotiable."

Katrina blinked. "I can't impose—"

"It's not imposing if I'm insisting." Edna's voice was firm. "Give Michelle time to get the doors fixed."

Emmett studied Katrina. "Most people in your situation would pack up and leave town. Aren't you from Atlanta?"

Everyone went quiet, waiting for her response. Katrina set down her fork. "I'm done running." The words hung in the air. She meant them.

Tracey reached over and squeezed her hand. "Good."

Emmett cleared his throat. "Well, speaking of not running..." He pulled the papers toward him. "I've been going through that contract you sent me. Want to hear some good news?"

Katrina's stomach knotted. "There's good news?"

"The contract is void."

She stared at him. "What?"

"Void as in worthless. Like it never existed." Emmett tapped the pages. "Julian lied to you about what LifeTrack actually was. He told you it was a wellness app to help people be more productive, right?"

"Right."

"But it is actually spyware. He was tracking your location, collecting your data, monitoring everything you did. That's not what you agreed to promote."

Katrina nodded slowly. "He never told me about any of that."

"Exactly. And that's called fraudulent inducement." Emmett leaned forward. "Basically, he tricked you into signing a contract by lying about what the product was. You signed up to promote a wellness app. What he gave you was a surveillance tool. Those are two completely different things."

"So the contract doesn't count?"

"Not only does it not count, but you had every legal right to walk away the moment you figured out what he was really doing. He violated multiple privacy laws with that app. This is textbook fraud."

"So I can't be sued for breach of contract?"

"No. Because you didn't breach anything. He did. From day one." Emmett's expression hardened. "Every time he threatened to sue you, that was just intimidation. He knew he didn't have a leg to stand on. He was trying to scare you into staying."

The relief was so intense Katrina felt dizzy.

Emmett added, "And if other influencers come forward with similar stories, there could be a class action lawsuit. You might not be the only one he did this to."

Katrina felt something loosen in her chest.

Julian, you and your app are going down!

Chapter 31

Sweetgrass Bed & Breakfast
Saturday, June 27 at 10:30 a.m.

Katrina sat on the front porch of Sweetgrass staring at the street but not really seeing it. Her mind was on Emmett's revelations about the contract with LifeTrack.

The contract. She'd been so stupid.

Julian had presented it casually over dinner, calling it a standard "partnership opportunity." LifeTrack was going to change how people connected, how they shared their lives. And he wanted her to be one of the first influencers to showcase it. The terms seemed straightforward. Post regularly. Engage with followers. Promote the app. In exchange, she'd received equity and a monthly stipend that was more than most of her sponsorships combined.

She'd signed it without a lawyer. Without even reading past the first few pages.

Just like she'd done with half her sponsorships with fashion brands and skincare companies. She'd gotten so used to the routine that she'd stopped being careful. Sign on the dotted line, cash the check, post the content. Easy money.

Except this time, the contract had buried clauses about data access, content ownership, and mandatory participation in "platform development." Julian had weaponized her carelessness. He'd known exactly what he was doing.

And she'd walked right into it.

She looked up and smiled as Ben pulled into the driveway. Her smile faltered when she saw Jenna in the passenger seat.

Oh no! She hoped they weren't bringing her bad news about Julian. Katrina knew he would have the best lawyers his money could buy. It was obvious Julian would do anything to keep that app going.

Ben stepped out onto the porch first. His eyes immediately went to her face. His jaw clenched when he saw the bruise, but he didn't say anything. He just moved to her side and sat down in the double rocker next to her.

"How are you?" His voice was low.

"I'm okay."

He didn't look convinced, but he let it go.

Jenna sat down in one of the other rockers.

Katrina asked nervously, "Is everything okay?"

"Yes." Jenna pulled out a notepad. "Julian Cross is in custody at the Beaufort County Detention Center. He was denied bail."

Katrina exhaled. She hadn't realized how much she needed to hear that.

"He's a flight risk," Jenna continued. "He has the resources to disappear, and he poses a danger to you. The judge wasn't taking any chances. He's not getting out."

"What are the charges?"

"Breaking and entering, stalking, assault—" Jenna gestured at Katrina's face. "Your injuries are documented. We also have unlawful surveillance. The FBI is preparing federal charges, which include the Computer Fraud and Abuse Act violations, wire fraud, and potentially conspiracy, depending on what the investors knew."

"LifeTrack was collecting far more data than was disclosed to users," Jenna said. "And the backend access shows Julian monitoring specific users. There's also evidence he sold data to third parties."

"The Horizon Capital investors are being questioned," Jenna continued. "Two of them are already lawyering up. We're building a case." Jenna exchanged a look with Ben. Her voice softened. "The Horizon Capital connection gave us new leads on Theo."

Ben had to look away. His jaw worked. Katrina reached over and took his hand. He gripped it tightly.

"What happens next?" Katrina asked. "For me?"

"Grand jury in two to three weeks. That's just a formality. I'm sure they'll indict. You'll need to testify at trial, which will probably be spring of next year. The FBI may need additional interviews as they build their case." Jenna closed her notepad. "But you're safe. Julian won't make bail. We're processing a restraining order. And your testimony could help other victims come forward."

"When can I get back into my house?"

"It should be released by the end of day tomorrow."

"Don't worry about the doors." Ben said. "I already talked to Michelle. I've suggested she get some new solid, steel doors and double locks. But it wouldn't hurt to get a security system too."

Katrina nodded slowly. "Thank you, Ben. And you too, Jenna. For everything."

Jenna smiled. "You did the hard part. You got yourself to safety. You asked for help. And we got him." She stifled a yawn, then smiled apologetically. "Sorry. It's been a long night." She stood, tucking her notepad into her bag. "I'm going to head upstairs and get some rest."

"Of course," Katrina said. "You've earned it."

"I'll check in with you both later." Jenna gave Ben a pointed look before heading inside. The screen door closed softly behind her, leaving Ben and Katrina alone on the porch.

Ben turned to look at her. "How are you? Really?"

Katrina met his eyes. "I don't know yet. Relieved. Exhausted. Still processing." She touched her bruised cheek gingerly. "But safe. For the first time in months, I actually feel safe."

His hand lifted slightly, as if he wanted to touch her face, then stopped. Instead, he gently took her hand. "Good." His voice was soft. "That's good."

His fingers tightened around hers.

She squeezed back.

It was real. Julian was in custody. The nightmare was over.

Saturday, June 27 at 11:46 a.m.

After Ben left, Katrina went up to the Green room to lie down. A few minutes later, there was a knock on the door. Katrina sat up, "Come in."

Edna opened the door, holding a leather book in her hand. "Hey, honey, I won't keep you long. I did some digging after you mentioned your mother's maiden name was Miles."

Katrina swung her legs off the bed. "You did?"

"I knew a Ruth Miles. She attended Second Baptist."

Katrina's breath caught. "My grandmother's name was Ruth."

Edna opened the album and flipped through the pages. "Is this her?"

Katrina looked at the photograph. A young Black woman, maybe twenty-two or twenty-three, stood in front of the church in a Sunday dress. She had her mother's smile.

"That's her," Katrina whispered. "That's my grandmother. She was beautiful."

Edna turned more pages. Church potlucks. Easter services. A group photo with a dozen smiling faces. "The Miles family was well-loved in this community."

“I talked to my aunt this morning,” Katrina said. “Aunt Lola. She and my mom both grew up here. After my grandmother died, they just didn’t come back.”

Edna nodded. “That’s how it is sometimes. After the death of a matriarch, everyone goes their separate ways. It can be hard without the one who held the family together.”

Katrina sighed. “I guess I can relate. It was hard after my parents died. All I had was Aunt Lola.”

Edna’s expression softened with understanding. “I'm so sorry, honey.” She paused, then her face brightened slightly. “But you know, you might have more family here than you realize.”

“What do you mean?”

“There’s someone you should meet.” Edna beamed. “Your mother’s cousin. Patricia Miles-Henderson. Everyone calls her Pat. She owns the Second Chance Consignment shop on Bay Street.”

“I have a cousin here?” Katrina felt dizzy.

“You have several cousins here, honey. I would have mentioned it earlier, but it didn't seem like the right time,” Edna gave that knowing look she had and lifted her phone. “The Miles family has deep roots in Beaufort. When you’re ready, I can call Pat. I’m sure she would love to meet you. Her shop is fabulous. Pat collects all kinds of wonderful things.”

“I’d love that!” Katrina thought for a moment. “When I left Atlanta, I thought I was just trying to get away from Julian. But maybe... maybe I was coming home.”

Edna placed her arm around her shoulder. "Sometimes the Lord guides our steps even when we can't see the path."

Chapter 32

Four Months Later
Beaufort, South Carolina

Katrina adjusted the ring light, checking the frame on her phone screen one more time. The white headboard from Edna's storage provided the perfect backdrop, just like she'd imagined when she first saw it. Her small desk sat against the adjacent wall, organized with her filming equipment, laptop, and the collection of plants she'd been slowly acquiring.

It looked like a scaled-down version of her old Atlanta setup, but better somehow. More authentic. More *her*.

She hit record on her phone, which was mounted on the small tripod Ben had helped her set up last week.

"Hey, everyone, Kat here. Welcome back to the Lowcountry house renovation series." She gestured to the space behind her. "Today I'm going to show you the final bedroom setup. As you can see, I kept the white and neutral theme, but added some pops of green with these plants. And yes, I'm trying really hard not to kill them."

She smiled at the camera, feeling that familiar comfort of talking to her followers. It had taken weeks to feel ready to turn the camera back on, to be visible again. But this time felt different.

"I found these amazing floating shelves at the local thrift store. Shoutout to Second Chances Consignment on Bay Street. They're tagged in my captions.

"I think they're going to be perfect for displaying some of the coastal artwork I've been collecting. But first, I need your help to decide on placement..."

She continued filming for another few minutes, keeping it light and natural. She wore no heavy makeup and her hair had grown long enough for mini twists. When she finished, she reviewed the footage quickly. Good enough. She'd edit it later tonight after Ben left.

Ben.

She glanced at the clock on her nightstand. He'd be here in twenty minutes.

Katrina saved the video file and moved to the kitchen, checking on the chicken marsala she had simmering on the stove. Cooking had become one of her unexpected joys over the past few months. After years of DoorDash and meal prep services, actually making food in her own kitchen felt grounding somehow.

The table was already set. She'd added a small vase of wildflowers from the farmers market and lit a candle that smelled like sea salt and sage.

Was it too much? Was she trying too hard?

They'd been dancing around whatever this was between them for weeks now. Ben came by almost every day, sometimes with updates about the case, sometimes just to check on her. They'd had coffee at the Dockside Cafe. Walked along the waterfront. Sat on her back porch talking until the mosquitoes drove them inside.

But they hadn't defined it. Hadn't put words to what was growing between them.

Tonight felt different though.

No one expected her to stay in this house after what happened. Michelle Carver was very upset about what happened. Not about the broken doors, but that she'd unnecessarily brought danger to Kat with her Facebook post.

That was all behind her, and both entry doors were fortified with proper deadbolts and a security system had been installed.

A knock at the front door made her heart leap for joy. Katrina wiped her hands on a dish towel and went to answer it.

Ben stood on her porch holding a bottle of wine and looking slightly nervous, which was adorable on a man his size. He'd traded his usual work clothes for dark jeans and a navy button-down shirt.

"Hey," he said. "You said casual, but I wasn't sure if I should've dressed up more—"

"You look perfect." The words came out before she could stop them, and she felt heat rise to her cheeks. "I mean, you look fine. Good. Come in."

He smiled that warm smile that had become her favorite thing over the past month. "Something smells amazing."

"Chicken marsala. I hope you like mushrooms; I may have gone overboard." She led him to the kitchen, suddenly nervous about the meal. "I haven't cooked for anyone in years. I'm probably rusty."

"I'm sure it's great." Ben set the wine on the counter. "And I brought this, though I don't actually know anything about wine. The guy at the store said it goes with chicken."

Katrina took the bottle—a respectable Pinot Grigio—and found herself smiling. "It's perfect."

They moved around the kitchen together with an easy familiarity that came from Ben spending so much time here over the past month. He found the wine opener in the drawer without asking. She grabbed glasses from the cabinet. They worked in comfortable silence while she plated the food.

Once they were seated at the small table, they began eating.

Ben asked casually without looking at her, "So you're really staying here in Beaufort?"

She smiled. "I have plenty of good reasons to stay."

He stared into her eyes. "I hope I'm one of those reasons."

"Of course."

Ben raised his glass. "To new beginnings."

“To new beginnings,” Katrina echoed, clinking her glass against his.

About the Author

Tyora Moody is the author of **Soul-Searching Mysteries,** which includes **cozy mystery, women sleuth mystery,** and **romantic suspense** under the Christian Fiction genre. Her book series include the Eugeena Patterson Mysteries, Joss Miller Mysteries, Lowcountry Secrets, Serena Manchester Mysteries, Reed Family Mysteries, and the Victory Gospel Mysteries.

When Tyora isn't working for a literary client, she's either loving on her cats, listening to an audiobook or podcast, binge-watching crime shows or Marvel movies, and of course, thinking about the next book.

To contact Tyora about reviewing her books or book club discussions, visit her online at TyoraMoody.com.

Join her newsletter at https://tyoramoody.substack.com/

Tyora Moody's Books

Eugeena Patterson Mysteries

Deep Fried Trouble, #1

Oven Baked Secrets, #2

Lemon Filled Disaster, #3

A Simmering Dilemma, #4

An Unsavory Mess, #5

A Spicy Predicament, #6

Marinated Conditions, #7

Eugeena Patterson Family Shorts

Shattered Dreams, #1

A Blended Family Christmas, #2

Falling in Love... Again!, #3

Joss Miller Mysteries

Double Mocha Blues, #1

A Latte Mayhem, #2

Mint-Flavored Trouble, #3
Steamy Espresso Secrets, #4

Serena Manchester Mysteries
Hostile Eyewitness, prequel
Bittersweet Motives, #1
Dangerous Confessions, #2
Waning Innocence, #3
Presumed Guilty, #4
Shifting Blame, #5

Lowcountry Secrets (Romantic Suspense)
The Homecoming, #1
The Reckoning, #2

Reed Family Mysteries
Broken Heart, #1
Troubled Heart, #2
Relentless Heart, #3
With All My Heart, #3.5
Faithful Heart, #4
Wounded Heart, #5

Victory Gospel Series (Mysteries)
When Rain Falls, #1
When Memories Fade, #2
When Perfection Fails, #3

Victory Gospel Shorts (Sweet Romance)
The Replacement Date, #1
Southern Delights, #2
When Love Finds Me, #3
Nobody's Replacement, #4
A Southern Delights Christmas, #5
Holding on to Love, #6

www.ingramcontent.com/pod-product-compliance
Lightning Source LLC
LaVergne TN
LVHW020705110826
845149LV00012B/2109

* 9 7 8 1 9 6 1 4 3 7 3 2 6 *